Keeping the

Faith

in the

Face of Fear

Carly Barone

ONE

The day was bright, and the air was filled with the sweet smell of strawberries as I walked through the busy lanes of the famous Florida Strawberry Festival. The colorful stalls showed off the creativity and community spirit, with local farmers proudly displaying their harvests and presenting crafts inspired by the festival's theme. I didn't usually like crowded places, but the excitement of the festival drew me in. I walked with my sister, Emma, as we chatted about each table we passed.

Emma had come to visit from California, and we hadn't seen each other in a couple of years because of her job, but we talked on the phone nearly every day. As we got close to a lively area near the music stage, my attention was caught by a young man chasing a mischievous straw hat blown by the wind. I watched in amazement as, with a quick and skillful jump, he caught the hat just before it almost hit me.

"Oops! Sorry about that," he said, with a sheepish grin spreading across his face as he straightened his hat back on his head.

"I'm Michael," he introduced himself, extending a hand.

I shook his hand, amused by the incident, and replied, smiling, "Evelyn."

"If you're up for it, I owe you a strawberry smoothie for almost taking you out with my hat," Michael suggested, pointing towards a nearby stand selling drinks.

The stand held a string of lights with vibrant banners showing the different smoothie choices.

"That sounds great," I accepted, and we made our way to the stand, as the crowd parted easily around us. The festival grounds were buzzing with the chatter of the visitors and the lively tunes of a jazz band playing in the distance. As Michael and I walked to get our smoothies, the colors of the sunset began to paint the sky, casting a soft golden light over the scene.

At the smoothie stand, Michael ordered two strawberry smoothies, his demeanor relaxed and friendly.

"You know, I think fate owes you more than just a smoothie for bringing us together like this," he joked as his eyes twinkled with humor.
I smirked at Michael's comment while enjoying the ease of our conversation.

"Maybe fate is just setting the scene," I giggled as I took the cool drink from the vendor. The first sip of my smoothie tasted rich and sweet, which was a perfect reflection of the day.

We walked a few yards away and chose a bench away from the main hustle, near a small grove of trees that provided a peaceful backdrop. As we sat, the noise of the festival seemed to fade into a gentle hum, giving us a quiet moment.

"So, Evelyn, what brings you to the festival today? Tradition, or something more adventurous?" Michael asked, genuinely interested.

"It was mostly my sister Emma's idea," I admitted, gesturing toward where my sister had mingled into the crowd.

"She loves these kinds of events. I usually prefer quieter weekends, but I'm glad I came. It's been a wonderful day." Michael nodded.

"I get that. I'm the opposite, though. I thrive in these settings—lots of people, energy, creativity floating around. It's inspiring for my work as a reporter, but thankfully it's my day off," he explained, his gaze reflecting his passion for his job. We continued to talk, delving into topics like our favorite artists, the quirkiest books we had read, and our most memorable vacations. Each topic opened a new avenue of conversation, revealing to each other more about our personalities and interests.

As the sky darkened and the festival lights began to shine brighter, Michael leaned slightly towards me, his expression thoughtful.

"You know, I'm really glad the wind decided to play matchmaker today," he said softly.

"Meeting you has been the highlight of this festival."

I felt a warmth spread through me, my cheeks felt flushed as I was touched by his sincerity.

"And I'm glad your hat decided to take flight," I responded, my voice light but sincere.

There was a moment of comfortable silence as we both took in the atmosphere, the sounds of the festival now a pleasant hum around us. Finally, Michael spoke up, a hint of anticipation in his voice.

"Evelyn, would it be too forward to ask if I could see you again? Maybe not at a busy festival, but somewhere we can talk more... just the two of us?" I met his gaze, my mind already made up.

"I'd like that," I said, my smile mirroring his.

"What about dinner?" Michael asked, seeming a little forward, but it didn't bother me.

"Dinner sounds perfect." We swapped phone numbers, sealing our plans. As we parted ways, the promise of a new beginning lingered in the air, like the sweet scent of strawberries on a warm summer evening.

After we met by chance at the festival, Michael and I started seeing each other all the time. Our dates varied from quiet dinners at cozy restaurants to weekend outings exploring local museums and parks. Each date helped us learn more about each other's lives and dreams.

One evening, we visited a local art gallery hosting an exhibition on impressionist paintings. As we moved from one painting to another, Michael shared his thoughts on the use of color and light, while I talked about the emotions each piece evoked in me. This shared experience not only deepened my appreciation for art but also for each other's perspectives.

Another memorable date was a day spent at a botanical garden. We walked hand-in-hand through rows of blooming flowers, discussing our favorite novels and authors, and stopping occasionally to admire the beauty around us. It was here, surrounded by nature, that I truly began to see a future with Michael.

The day was unusually warm for early autumn, with a gentle breeze rustling through the leaves of the old oak tree under which Michael had spread a soft, checkered blanket. The park was quiet, a stark contrast to the bustling festival where Michael and I had first met. Here, surrounded by the whispers of the grass and the peaceful sounds of nature, Michael planned to propose to me.

I arrived at the park after using the restroom, and my heart fluttered with anticipation. I didn't know what to expect, but I was feeling the weight of the moment. Michael greeted me with his warm, reassuring smile, the one that had melted my worries away since the day we met. We shared a light picnic, savoring homemade sandwiches and fresh lemonade, chatting about trivial things that filled our daily lives. Yet, beneath our casual chat, there was a thrill, a tangible excitement brimming with promise.

As the sun began to lower, casting long shadows across the grass, Michael's demeanor shifted. He became quieter, more contemplative as if he were gathering his thoughts for something momentous. I noticed the change, and my curiosity piqued, my heart started racing with a mix of nervousness and excitement.

Finally, Michael turned to face me, taking my hands in his. His eyes, usually so full of laughter, now held a depth of seriousness mixed with a sparkle of joy.

"Evelyn," he began, his voice a soft murmur that was almost drowned out by the gentle breeze,

"From the moment we met, there was something magical between us. These past two months have been the most joyful of my life. I find myself falling deeper in love with you every day, and it's a journey I never want to end."

He paused, reaching into his bag and pulling out a small, velvet box. As he opened it, the late afternoon sun caught on the diamond ring inside, making it sparkle brilliantly. I gasped softly, my hands flying to my mouth in surprise.

"Evelyn, I know this might seem fast, but like I've always heard, when you know, you know. And I know, without a shadow of a doubt, that I want to spend every remaining day of my life with you."
His voice was steady, each word infused with sincerity.

"Will you marry me?"

Tears filled my eyes. I felt joy, surprise, and a strong feeling that everything was perfect.

I looked into Michael's eyes, seeing my future, our future reflected at me. With a voice choked with emotion, I whispered,

"Yes, Michael, yes. A thousand times, yes."

Michael slipped the ring onto my finger, our eyes locked in a moment of profound connection. We embraced, the world around us fading into a blur, as we held each other in the heart of the park that had seen the beginning of our story. The moment was ours alone, a cherished memory we would hold close to our hearts forever.

As we eventually pulled away, the sunset painted the sky in hues of gold and pink, a perfect backdrop to the new chapter we were beginning. The evening ended with laughter and plans, dreams of our future life together weaving through our conversation like threads of gold.

After the proposal, Michael and I chose a date for our wedding. We wanted a date that held significance for both of us, perhaps a season or month that carried sentimental value. After careful consideration, we settled on a date in early summer, a time of new beginnings and abundant growth.

Michael and I spent weekends touring various venues, from charming countryside estates to elegant city hotels. We were drawn to a charming little vineyard set among the rolling hills, where its scenic views made the perfect setting for our celebration. With the venue secured, we turned our attention to designing the wedding invitations. We wanted them to reflect our personalities and the style of our wedding—classic yet simple, with a touch of fun. Together, we spent evenings sketching designs and choosing fonts until we found the perfect combination.

One of the most enjoyable tasks was tasting the menu options for the reception. We sat down with the chef, sampling a variety of dishes from gourmet appetizers to delicious desserts. I enjoyed every bite, and we had fun talking about which dish was the best.

Music was another important part of our wedding day. We spent evenings creating playlists, picking songs that held special meaning for us as a couple. From the first dance to the last goodbye, every moment was planned to create just the right feeling.

Michael and I each set out to find the perfect outfits for the event. I spent hours trying on wedding gowns, searching for the one that made me feel like a princess. Meanwhile, Michael looked for a suit that struck the balance between classic elegance and modern style.

One of the most intimate moments in the wedding planning process was writing our vows. We set aside an evening to reflect on our love and commitment to each other, pouring our hearts into crafting words that captured the depth of our feelings. As we read our vows to each other, tears of joy and love flowed freely.

In the weeks leading up to the wedding, we attended to the final details, from seating arrangements to floral arrangements. There were moments of stress and tension, but we navigated through them together, our love and shared vision for the day guiding us through.

As the wedding day got closer, Michael and I found ourselves filled with a mixture of excitement and nervousness. We couldn't wait to exchange vows and begin our journey as husband and wife, but we also cherished the moments leading up to the big day—the quiet evenings spent together, the stolen glances filled with anticipation, and the knowledge that our love would soon be celebrated by all those closest to us.

With the wedding details meticulously planned and our hearts full of love and excitement, Michael and I were ready to start the next chapter of our lives together. The wedding day promised to be a celebration of our love, surrounded by family and friends who supported us on our journey.

On the wedding day, the air was charged with anticipation as Michael and I prepared to exchange vows and start a new chapter of our lives together.

The morning of the wedding dawned with a soft golden light, casting a warm glow over the vineyard where we would soon say our vows. In separate rooms, we began our preparations surrounded by our loved ones.

My bridesmaids flew around me like butterflies, making sure my hair and makeup looked just right. Emma, my maid of honor, helped me into my beautiful gown and put delicate pearls in my hair. My heart fluttered with excitement and nerves, my thoughts consumed by the promise of the day ahead.

Across the vineyard, Michael stood surrounded by his groomsmen, adjusting his tie with a mixture of excitement and anticipation. He stole glances at his watch, counting down the minutes until he would see me walk down the aisle.

The ceremony took place in a serene clearing within the vineyard, surrounded by rows of lush grapevines and towering oak trees. A rustic wooden arch adorned with billowing white fabric framed the altar, creating a romantic backdrop for the occasion.

The gentle strains of a string quartet signaled the start of the procession. My bridesmaids, dressed in flowing pastel gowns, made their way down the aisle, their steps synchronized with the rhythm of the music. Each carried a bouquet of wildflowers, adding a pop of color to the green surroundings.

As the music swelled, all eyes turned to me, breathtaking in my ivory lace gown. I walked gracefully down the aisle, my father's arm linked with mine, my heart racing with anticipation.

Against the backdrop of swaying vines and the soft murmur of the breeze, Michael and I stood hand in hand, ready to declare our love and commitment before our loved ones.

Our vows, spoken from the heart, echoed through the clearing, each word a promise of enduring love and unwavering support. Tears of joy glistened in our eyes as we exchanged rings, symbols of our eternal bond. With a soft sigh, we sealed our vows with a tender kiss, the clearing erupting into applause and cheers. As we turned to face our guests, the officiant smiled warmly, pronouncing us husband and wife to the delight of all present.

Following the ceremony, guests made their way to the reception area, where tables adorned with flickering candles and floral centerpieces awaited them. Soft music filled the air, setting a relaxed and festive atmosphere. Michael and I greeted each guest with heartfelt thanks and warm hugs. Our joy was contagious as we mingled and shared laughs with our family and friends.

As dinner was served, heartfelt toasts and speeches were shared. Each one was a testament to the love and admiration felt for us. Tears of laughter and sentiment flowed freely as stories were told and memories were shared.

The highlight of the evening was our first dance as husband and wife. With the gentle strains of our favorite song filling the air, we moved together with grace and elegance, lost in the moment and the love we shared.

Throughout the evening, there were countless special moments—father-daughter dances, impromptu sing-alongs, and heartfelt conversations shared under the starlit sky. Each moment added to the magic of the night and the memories that would last a lifetime.

After the whirlwind of the wedding festivities, Michael and I escaped to a secluded villa on the shores of a tropical paradise. Surrounded by palm trees and crystal-clear waters, we found the perfect setting for relaxation and romance.

During our honeymoon, Michael and I enjoyed a variety of romantic activities, from sunset cruises along the coastline to private dinners under the stars. Each day brought new adventures and cherished moments as we enjoyed each other's company.

As we lounged on the beach, our toes buried in the sand, we took the time to reflect on our future together. We talked about our hopes and dreams, our aspirations for starting a family, and the adventures we would take as a married couple. Away from the pressures of daily life, Michael and I reconnected on a deeper level, strengthening the bond that had brought us together. We laughed, we talked, and we fell more deeply in love with each passing day.

With the ceremony, reception, and honeymoon now cherished memories, we returned home ready to embrace the next chapter of our lives together. Little did we know, our journey was about to take an unexpected turn.

Several months after our honeymoon, I began to notice subtle changes in my body—a slight queasiness in the mornings, and a sudden craving for pickles and ice cream. At first, I dismissed those signs as mere quirks, but as the weeks passed, I couldn't shake the feeling that something was different.

One morning, I was woken by a wave of nausea. I decided to take a pregnancy test, and as I waited for the results, my heart raced with anticipation. When the test displayed two bold lines, confirming my suspicions, my breath got caught in my throat. I was pregnant.

After Michael and I received the initial confirmation of my pregnancy, we couldn't wait to share the news with our families and friends. We planned a special dinner, inviting our loved ones to celebrate what they thought was the arrival of our first child.

As everyone gathered around the table, Michael and I exchanged knowing glances, our excitement bubbling just beneath the surface. With a shared look, we raised our glasses, signaling that we had something important to announce.

With a nervous smile, I stood up, my hands trembling slightly as I held onto Michael for support. I began by recounting the journey that led us to this moment—our love story, our wedding, and the joy of discovering my pregnancy.

Then, with a dramatic pause, I revealed the double surprise that awaited us.

"But there's more," I said, my voice trembling with emotion.

"We're not just expecting one baby... we're expecting two. We're having twins."

The room erupted into cheers and applause, the news of twins sparking an outpouring of excitement and disbelief. Tears of pure happiness streamed down my cheeks as I looked around at the faces of our loved ones, each one offering their love and support.

Michael wrapped his arms around me, holding me close as we basked in the warmth of our family's embrace. At that moment, surrounded by the people we loved most, we felt very grateful and happy.

In the days following our news of expecting twins, we experienced a whirlwind of emotions—joy, excitement, and a healthy dose of apprehension. The thought of raising two babies at once was daunting, but we knew that together, we could handle anything.

We spent countless hours researching twin pregnancies, stocking up on baby supplies, and preparing our home for the arrival of our little ones. With each passing day, our anticipation grew, mingled with a healthy dose of nervousness and wonder.

Michael and I threw ourselves into preparing for the arrival of our twins, transforming the spare room into a cozy nursery filled with two cribs, changing tables, and a mountain of adorable baby clothes. We spent evenings assembling furniture and decorating the walls with fun designs.

As we worked side by side, Michael and I found comfort in being together. Our shared excitement erased any doubts or fears we had. We talked about the kind of parents we wanted to be and our hopes and dreams for our growing family.

With each passing week, my belly grew rounder, a visible reminder of the miracle happening inside me. We went to prenatal appointments together, listening with awe as the doctor showed us the movements of our twins on the ultrasound screen.

When we felt the first kicks and flutters, we marveled at the bond we already had with our unborn babies. We talked to them, sang to them, and dreamed about the day we would finally hold them in our arms.

As my pregnancy progressed and our preparations continued, Michael and I eagerly looked forward to the arrival of our twins, knowing that our lives were about to change in the most beautiful and profound ways. Together, we started our journey of parenthood, filled with love, laughter, and the endless joys of family.

TWO

As Michael and I arrived at the hospital, I felt excitement and nerves running through me. We walked hand in hand through the halls, my steps steady despite the butterflies in my stomach. Michael squeezed my hand, his eyes full of love and excitement.

When we entered the labor and delivery unit, the nurses greeted us with warm smiles and guided us to our room with gentle reassurances. The room was softly lit, with the hum of medical equipment and the distant sounds of other laboring mothers in the background.

I settled into the hospital bed, surrounded by soft pillows and cozy blankets. These comforts eased my physical pains and brought a familiar sense of security, reminding me of home. Michael stayed by my side, his presence a steady and reassuring force amid the whirlwind of emotions. Even with the uncertainty and the hustle of the doctors and nurses around us, his calmness kept me grounded. His hand, warm and firm, held mine, offering quiet encouragement and support.

The room, with its soft beeping machines and the quiet steps of nurses, all seemed to fade away as I focused on the comfort of the blankets and the strength I drew from Michael being there. His unwavering support was my rock, reminding me that no matter what challenges we faced, we weren't facing them alone. This deepened our bond, strengthening our connection at a time when I needed it the most.

As the hours passed, my labor moved forward with a steady, unyielding rhythm. Each contraction surged through me with intense power, a vivid reminder of the incredible miracle that was unfolding. The pain was deep, but the purpose behind it was even deeper, pushing me closer to the moment I would meet my child.

With every contraction, I felt the overwhelming intensity of the process. Yet, I found strength within myself, fortified by Michael's unwavering support. He was my constant companion through each wave of pain, his presence calming and encouraging. His words were soft and uplifting, reminding me of the joy that awaited us, and his touch was tender, a soothing balm against the sharp stings of each contraction.

Michael held my hand tightly, his eyes often meeting mine with a look of deep empathy and admiration. With every soothing word and gentle touch, he helped ease my discomfort, making the challenging moments more bearable. His encouragement was a powerful antidote to the fear and fatigue that threatened to overwhelm me. This partnership, this shared journey through the trials of labor, underscored the depth of our connection and the strength of our bond.

Together, Michael and I faced each contraction, growing closer with each passing moment. This shared experience deepened our relationship, each surge bringing us closer to the life we would soon welcome into the world. The medical team monitored me and the twins closely, their expertise and professionalism instilling confidence in both of us. They adjusted the monitors, checked my vitals, and prepared the delivery equipment with quiet efficiency, ready to spring into action at a moment's notice.

When the decision was made for me to have a cesarean section, I gathered all my strength and courage. Though this wasn't the birth scenario I had initially imagined, my focus remained firm, driven by the imminent joy of meeting my babies. Lying on the operating table, I felt a mix of nervous anticipation and excitement. Each preparation by the medical team brought me closer to the moment I would finally see my precious little ones.

With Michael by my side, holding my hand, I felt reassured despite the clinical environment and the buzz of activity. His presence allowed me to stay calm and have strength, helping me stay positive. As the doctors worked, I focused on the incredible outcome to come: the first cries of my babies and seeing their faces for the first time. This anticipation filled me with excitement, reminding me that each moment now was a step toward meeting my new family.

Evette's arrival into the world brought a fresh wave of emotion. Her first breaths were marked by tears of joy and cheers from the medical team and my family. The room buzzed with happiness and relief as this new life joined our family.

The nurses gently cleaned and wrapped Evette in a soft, warm blanket and placed her in my arms. Holding my daughter for the first time, I was awestruck by the delicate features of the tiny miracle nestled against my chest. Evette's skin was soft and warm, her tiny hands moved with a curious grace, and her little eyes fluttered open as if aware of the significance of this first meeting.

When Evette's eyes met mine, there was a moment of profound connection. In my daughter's gaze, I saw a flicker of recognition, a spark of shared understanding that seemed to say,

"Here I am, Mom." The wonder in Evette's eyes mirrored the awe and love swelling within my heart.

This magical encounter deepened our bond instantly, sealing a connection that would only grow with time. I marveled at my daughter, feeling immense gratitude and a protective instinct that surged through me with every tiny heartbeat I felt against my own. The room seemed to quiet down for those few moments, focusing all attention on the beautiful, serene connection between mother and daughter.

Moments later, the room filled with the joyous sound of Elijah's first cries as he made his entrance into the world. His arrival brought a wave of relief and excitement from everyone present. Although he was smaller than expected, Elijah's voice was strong and clear, ringing out like a triumphant anthem. His cries echoed around the room, infusing the space with the sweet music of new beginnings.

The medical team efficiently and gently cared for him, wrapping him in a soft blanket, but all eyes were on the tiny figure whose presence was a profound reassurance. His vitality and the vigorous sound of his crying were comforting confirmations of his health and spirit. Michael squeezed my hand a little tighter, our shared smiles filled with wonder and joy.

As Michael and I gazed down at our newborn twins, our hearts swelled with love and gratitude. We marveled at the tiny fingers and toes, the delicate features that mirrored our own, and the overwhelming joy that filled the room like sunlight breaking through the clouds on a stormy day.

In the first two years after Evette and Elijah were born, Michael and I embraced the wonders and challenges of parenthood. Each day brought new reasons to smile and marvel as we watched our twins grow and develop. We found immense joy in witnessing each of their 'firsts'—moments that captured the fleeting nature of childhood and the deep, enduring love of a parent.

From the very first time Evette and Elijah flashed their gummy smiles, my heart swelled with pride and wonder. Those smiles soon turned into giggles, filling our home with the sound of joy and marking the beginning of countless playful days. When the twins began to explore the world on their own, first by crawling and then taking their first steps, Michael and I were always there, ready with open arms and encouraging words. Each little step was celebrated as a major victory, a testament to the twins' growing independence and curiosity.

Michael and I kept a cherished collection of these milestones. We took photos and videos and wrote down memories in a special book for the twins' early years. We shared these achievements with family and friends, our pride clear in our wide smiles and excited stories. Each new skill and discovery was not just a step forward for the twins but also a moment for us to realize the profound journey of parenting.

These years were filled with more than just developmental milestones; they were rich with moments of bonding, learning, and discovery. Whether it was quiet evenings reading books together, afternoons in the park, or just cuddling under a blanket, each moment was full of love and the deep satisfaction of family life. Michael and I cherished every day, knowing that these early years were laying the foundation for the lifelong bond we would share with our children.

However, as Elijah approached his second birthday, Michael and I began to notice subtle differences in his development. He struggled to sit up by himself, his movements hesitant and uncoordinated. While Evette thrived, reaching each milestone with ease, Elijah's progress seemed slower.

With a mix of concern and hope, Michael and I noticed that Elijah's development was different from Evette's. His responses to social cues were less pronounced, and he reached milestones at a noticeably slower pace. Wanting the best for our son and seeking clarity, we decided to consult our pediatrician for advice.

During the appointment, we shared our observations and concerns with the pediatrician, who listened attentively and provided a calming presence. The pediatrician conducted a preliminary assessment of Elijah, observing his interactions and motor skills. Based on these observations, he suggested that it would be wise to seek a more comprehensive evaluation to understand Elijah's developmental delays better.

The recommendation was for specialists—like a developmental pediatrician and possibly a neurologist—to assess Elijah to get a clearer understanding of his needs. The pediatrician explained that this evaluation would be thorough, involving a series of tests and observations to help identify any underlying conditions and guide us toward the most effective interventions.

Michael and I felt reassured, knowing we were taking proactive steps to support our son. The pediatrician's gentle and informative approach made us feel more hopeful about understanding Elijah's unique needs and ensuring he received the appropriate support to thrive.

We left the office with a referral and a clear plan for our next steps. This was my promise to do whatever it took to help Elijah thrive.

The diagnosis of cerebral palsy came as a shock to Michael and me. We struggled to come to terms with the reality of our son's condition. The medical team reassured us, providing information and resources to help us navigate Elijah's journey.

In addition to cerebral palsy, Elijah also underwent evaluations for autism spectrum disorder, as his developmental delays and difficulties with social communication raised concerns. While the results were inconclusive at the time, I was determined to ensure Elijah had everything he needed to succeed.

From the moment Elijah was born, Michael was filled with pride and joy, unlike anything he had ever experienced. He cradled our newborn son in his arms, marveling at the tiny fingers and button nose that mirrored his own. To Michael, Elijah was perfect in every way.

When I first brought up the subject of Elijah's developmental delays, Michael brushed off my concerns with a confident smile. He saw Elijah as simply taking his time to catch up with his sister, Evette, and dismissed any notion that there could be something wrong.

As I scheduled appointments with doctors and specialists, Michael reluctantly accompanied me, his skepticism evident in the furrow of his brow and the set of his jaw. He listened to the doctors' assessments with growing unease, refusing to acknowledge the possibility that Elijah might have special needs.

When the doctors suggested further evaluations and tailored interventions for Elijah, Michael's initial reaction was one of resistance and frustration. As he listened to the doctor's recommendations, he was in disbelief and anger began to build within him. He questioned the necessity of such extensive assessments, convinced that the doctors might be exaggerating Elijah's developmental challenges or misunderstanding his behaviors.

Michael's frustration showed as a simmering tension that was hard to miss. He expressed his doubts openly, challenging the doctors' expertise and their approach. He wondered aloud whether these evaluations were truly in Elijah's best interest or if they were simply part of a cautious, perhaps overly cautious, medical protocol. His voice carried a mix of concern and skepticism, reflecting his internal struggle to reconcile professional advice with his observations and instincts as a father.

This reaction came from a place of deep concern for his son but also from a fear of what such evaluations might mean for Elijah's future. Michael worried about labeling his son at such a young age, fearing that it might limit him rather than help him. He grappled with the idea, uncomfortable with the thought of subjecting Elijah to a long series of tests and interventions that might not even be necessary.

Despite his resistance, I tried to calm his worries, suggesting we gather all the information and perspectives before making any decisions. I hoped that by understanding more about Elijah's needs, we could better support his development and ensure he had every opportunity to thrive. Michael, though hesitant, agreed to think it over, his love for his son pushing him to consider all possibilities, even those that initially unsettled him.

Michael's denial put a strain on our relationship. I struggled to settle with his refusal to accept Elijah's diagnosis with my concerns for our son's well-being. I pleaded with Michael to see reason, to acknowledge Elijah's needs, and to seek the help he deserved.

Our once harmonious partnership became filled with tension and disagreement. My pleas fell on deaf ears as Michael retreated further into his denial. He resented my insistence on seeking help for Elijah, viewing it as an attack on his abilities as a father.

It wasn't until a particularly challenging therapy session, where Elijah's struggles were clear, that Michael's denial finally broke. As he watched his son grapple with tasks that came easily to other children, Michael felt a surge of helplessness and despair.

At that moment, the weight of his denial became too heavy to bear. He realized that by refusing to acknowledge Elijah's challenges, he was only hindering his son's ability to get the support and care he needed. With a heavy heart, Michael began to confront the reality of Elijah's diagnosis and his role in his son's journey.

Despite the initial shock and uncertainty that surrounded the diagnosis, I found a well of strength within myself to support Elijah fully. I enveloped him in love and encouragement, determined to be his pillar as he embarked on his challenging journey of growth and discovery. Learning that Elijah's cerebral palsy primarily affected his gross motor skills brought clarity but also a roadmap of the difficulties we would face together.

Elijah struggled with basic physical movements like sitting, standing, and walking on his own. His muscles were unusually rigid due to stiffness and spasticity, which not only hindered his freedom of movement but often led to discomfort and frustration. I could see how these physical limitations affected him, not just physically but also emotionally, as he faced the barriers that set him apart from other children his age.

With unwavering determination, I sought out therapies and aids that could ease his discomfort and improve his mobility. I was always there, right beside him during his therapy sessions, offering words of encouragement and celebrating even the smallest progress. I made it my mission to fill his world with joy and positivity, reinforcing that his values and capabilities were not defined by his physical challenges.

Together, we explored every avenue that could provide relief and support, from physical therapy to adaptive equipment that could help Elijah gain more independence. Each step on this path, though challenging, was also filled with moments of triumph and deep bonding. My nurturing presence and steadfast support became the backbone of Elijah's journey, a constant reminder that he was not alone in his challenges.

Alongside the challenges with his gross motor skills, Elijah also faced difficulties with his fine motor skills, which affected his ability to handle smaller, more precise movements. Tasks that required fine motor control, like grasping objects or manipulating small items, were particularly tough for him. Simple everyday actions, such as holding a spoon during mealtime or picking up a toy to play with, presented significant hurdles that he had to overcome.

For Elijah, these activities weren't just physically demanding; they required a lot of concentration and patience. Every attempt to grip a spoon tightly enough to scoop food, or to clasp a small toy in his hands, tested his persistence and resilience. These moments, while challenging, were also filled with opportunities for learning and growth. I saw each struggle not just as a difficulty but as a chance for him to develop new skills through practice and encouragement.

I worked closely with Elijah's therapists to weave fun and engaging exercises into our daily routine to improve his dexterity. We used a variety of tools and activities, like play dough to strengthen his hand muscles, or large beads and strings for him to thread, turning these tasks into playful learning experiences. I always made sure to frame these activities positively, cheering Elijah on with each small success and encouraging him to enjoy the process rather than focusing solely on the outcome.

Through our dedicated efforts, every small victory in Elijah's ability to manipulate objects bolstered his confidence. Despite the slow progress, the joy in his eyes when he managed to hold something on his own was a profound reward for both of us. My patient and persistent support played a crucial role in helping Elijah navigate these challenges, reminding him that with time and practice, he could achieve more independence.

Speech and language development posed another hurdle for Elijah, as he struggled to communicate his needs and express himself verbally. While he understood simple instructions and commands, his ability to form words and sentences was limited, leading to frustration and meltdowns.

THREE

As the twins' fourth birthday approached, my heart ached with concern as I saw the growing distance between Michael and Elijah. Each passing day seemed to widen the gap, leaving me feeling helpless and in despair. My instincts screamed at me to protect Elijah from the pain of rejection radiating from his father. I couldn't bear to see my son's once bright eyes clouded with confusion and hurt, his innocence shattered by Michael's cold indifference.

Talking to Michael about Elijah's challenges and the need for consistent support was difficult for me. Every conversation felt like walking a tightrope, where each word I chose carried immense weight—the weight of my unspoken fears for our son's future and the shattered dreams that lingered between us. It required a careful balance, trying not to trigger a defensive response while still communicating the urgency and importance of the situation.

As I brought up the topic, I saw Michael's demeanor change almost instantly. His expression hardened, and his posture stiffened as if he were physically building a wall around himself. It was as if with each word I spoke, I could see the bricks being laid, his defenses rising like a fortress designed to shut out the difficult truths I was trying to convey.

Michael's reluctance to fully acknowledge the extent of Elijah's pain and the implications it carried for our family life was deeply painful for me to witness. It felt as though he was not only distancing himself from the responsibilities but also from the emotional reality of our son's experiences. This refusal was like a dagger to my heart, each evasion a signal of his unwillingness to face the challenges head-on, together as a family.

Watching this unfold, I felt a mixture of frustration, sadness, and desperation. I needed Michael not just as a co-parent but as a partner who could share in the emotional burden, who could understand and acknowledge the pain and the hope wrapped up in Elijah's daily struggles. The gap his stance created was not just about differing views on treatment or therapy; it was a chasm that touched the very core of our relationship, highlighting a disconnect that went beyond mere words and into the realms of empathy and support.

Elijah's confusion was palpable, a heavy fog that enveloped him like a suffocating embrace. He couldn't understand why his father no longer looked at him with the same warmth and affection, why his once playful gestures now felt like shards of ice against his skin.

As a small child, Elijah was deeply affected by the complexities of his relationship with his father, Michael. Though still young, he could feel the emotional distance that had grown between them. His heart, innocent and yearning for affection, felt the weight of what seemed like rejection. Elijah often looked up with wide, questioning eyes, silently searching for answers to why his father's attention seemed so elusive.

Elijah longed for the simple joys of fatherly affection—being scooped up into Michael's arms, feeling the secure embrace that spoke of safety and unconditional love. He dreamed of those moments when paternal warmth would envelop him, providing comfort and reassurance amidst his daily struggles with cerebral palsy. However, these moments were rare, and more often than not, he felt as though he was on the periphery of Michael's world, overlooked and unimportant, like a piece of yesterday's news that had lost its relevance.

This feeling of being set aside left Elijah grappling with feelings of inadequacy and confusion. At times, he would watch other children with their fathers and wonder why his interactions were so different. The lack of warmth and connection from Michael contrasted sharply with the loving care he received from me, creating a painful disparity in his young heart.

Despite this, Elijah tried to maintain hope, occasionally reaching out with small gestures—a smile, a word, an outstretched hand—each one a silent plea for recognition and love. Yet, with each day that passed with minimal response, the hope dimmed slightly, leaving him to wrestle with the complex emotions of feeling unwanted and uncherished by someone who was supposed to be his protector and hero.

Michael's defiance was like a slap in the face, a cruel reminder of the man he once was and the father he had become. He refused to acknowledge my concerns, dismissing them as overblown and unnecessary, blind to the pain he was inflicting on his flesh and blood.

In moments of frustration and stubbornness, Michael's demeanor took a harsh turn toward me, his words becoming sharp and cutting. During these exchanges, his language was heavy with venom and contempt, an outward expression of his inner turmoil and defensiveness. He harshly accused me of babying Elijah, of coddling him too much, which he argued was only making his dependencies and weaknesses worse. His accusations were fierce, suggesting that my nurturing was a disservice to our son's development, rather than seeing it as the supportive love it was intended to be.

Michael's unwillingness to acknowledge his part in Elijah's life—his absence, both emotionally and physically—added a layer of blame and unfair criticism directed towards me. He refused to see or accept his shortcomings as a father, instead projecting his frustrations on me, claiming I was the problem rather than facing the more painful truth of his lack of involvement.

This behavior created a painful rift between us. Each argument left deeper scars and widened the gap of understanding and cooperation that was so crucial for Elijah's care. I, for my part, bore the brunt of these accusations with a mix of sadness and resilience. I knew the truth of my son's needs and the genuine love behind my actions. While Michael's harsh words hurt, they only strengthened my resolve to provide Elijah with the emotional and physical support he needed.

As these confrontations grew more frequent, the tension in our relationship became a palpable presence, casting a shadow over our interactions and complicating the family dynamics. This ongoing struggle not only affected our partnership but also the emotional climate of our home, making it a challenging environment for everyone, especially Elijah, who was sensitive to the undercurrents of discord.

As the days turned into weeks, Elijah's heartache deepened, a yawning chasm of emptiness that threatened to consume him whole. He watched with longing as Evette basked in her father's attention, her laughter a mocking echo of the love he so desperately craved.

My heart broke as I witnessed the profound impact Michael's distant behavior had on Elijah. Day by day, I saw my son retreating further into himself, his usual bright and vibrant spirit overshadowed by growing sadness and confusion. The lively spark that once lit up his eyes began to fade, dimmed by the heavy weight of feeling unaccepted by his father.

Watching this transformation was excruciating. I saw the wonder in Elijah's eyes, the silent questions about why his father seemed so distant toward him and why his efforts to connect were met with indifference. This rejection was something no child should have to feel, especially from a parent, and it tore at my heart to see my son grappling with such pain.

In response, I did what I knew best—I offered Elijah the comfort and security of my embrace. I held him close, wrapping him in my arms, a haven of warmth and softness against the harshness of his emotional turmoil. My hugs were more than just physical support; they were a silent message of unconditional love and acceptance, telling him that no matter what, he was cherished and valued.

As I soothed my son, whispering words of love and encouragement, I felt a fierce determination grow within me. I became more resolved to shield Elijah from the negative impacts of his father's rejection and to reinforce the positive, loving energy in his life. My embrace was not just a comfort but a fortress, guarding him against the storm of emotions raging within him and helping him to hold onto the light that his father's actions had threatened to extinguish.

I whispered words of reassurance and love, promising to always be there for him no matter what. I vowed to shield him from the pain of rejection that may come. Three days after the twin's fourth birthday, our house buzzed with anticipation as I meticulously prepared for their joint birthday party. Streamers adorned the walls, balloons bobbed cheerfully in the air, and a colorful array of decorations brightened every corner of the room.

With a heart full of love and determination, I threw myself into the preparations with gusto. I adorned the walls with colorful streamers and hung strings of twinkling fairy lights from the ceiling, creating a magical atmosphere that sparkled with excitement and anticipation.

With the kitchen counter overflowing with baking supplies and my imagination soaring, I set out to create a birthday cake not just to mark another year, but to make a magical memory. My hands, skilled and steady from years of practice, picked through an array of colorful sprinkles, various shades of icing, and multiple flavors of cake mix, each component ready to play its part in the day's creation.

My plan was for a cake that was more than just dessert—it was to be a centerpiece, a visual celebration of joy and creativity. As I mixed and measured, I envisioned a cake that would look like it had leaped from the pages of a children's fairytale, where whimsy and wonder ruled. I chose to adorn the cake with sugary flowers, each petal crafted with care, the colors vibrant against the soft hue of the cake's icing.

The construction of the cake was meticulous. Layers of fluffy, moist sponge were stacked with precision, with the edges aligned perfectly. Between each layer, I spread a generous amount of rich, creamy frosting, adding flavor and stability in equal measure. Once the layers were assembled, I coated the entire structure in a thin layer of icing, creating a smooth canvas for my decorative skills to shine.

My delicate touch then came into play as I piped intricate designs along the sides and across the top of the cake. The icing was applied with an artist's precision, swirling and looping into elegant patterns that encapsulated the enchantment of a fairytale. Atop this, the sugary flowers were placed with care, each one a testament to my attention to detail and my desire to make something truly beautiful.

As I stepped back to admire my work, the cake stood tall and proud on the kitchen counter—a masterpiece of baking that looked like the creations found in storybooks. It was more than I had hoped for, a perfect blend of my skill and my heart, made not just to feed the guests at the party but to feed their imaginations as well.

While I worked tirelessly to bring my vision to life, Michael lounged on the couch, his eyes glued to the television screen as he sipped on a beer. Oblivious to the chaos unfolding around him, he remained unaware of the effort and dedication it took to organize such a grand affair.

With each passing hour, my frustration grew. My heart was heavy with disappointment as I watched Michael waste the precious moments leading up to the party. I had hoped for his support and encouragement, but instead, I was met with indifference and apathy.

Alone in my efforts to organize a memorable celebration, I showed resilience and determination. As I moved through the tasks of setting up for the party, my resolve never wavered, even as I encountered one challenge after another. With each new obstacle, whether it was a tangled string of lights or a shortage of tape, I found a solution, my creativity and resourcefulness coming to the fore.

I hung banners across the room, each one carefully measured and placed to create a festive atmosphere. My hands, though growing weary, moved with the precision and skill of someone who had done this many times before. Each banner was smoothed and secured, ensuring that the decorations looked cheerful and welcoming.

Next, I turned my attention to the balloons. With a pump in hand, I inflated each one, tying them off with nimble fingers. I chose a variety of colors to match the party theme, and soon, clusters of floating balloons added to the room's charm. Despite the physical strain, my movements remained graceful and efficient, a testament to my experience and unwavering focus on the task at hand.

As the hours passed, exhaustion began to creep up on me. My back ached from the constant bending and reaching, and my hands felt stiff from tying countless knots. Yet, I pushed these discomforts aside, driven by a deep desire to give my children the joyous celebration they deserved. The thought of their smiles and the laughter that would soon fill the room gave me a surge of energy, a reminder of why every effort was worth it.

My commitment to creating a perfect day for my children was evident in every detail of the preparation. I knew that these moments would become cherished memories for my family, and this knowledge fueled me to keep going, to make everything as beautiful and joyful as possible. My love for my children was the force that kept me moving forward, ensuring that despite the fatigue, I would not relent. I was determined to create a day filled with happiness and love, and nothing was going to stand in my way.

As the party got underway, it became clear that Michael's attention was solely focused on Evette. He hovered near her, showering her with gifts and praise, while barely sparing a glance for Elijah, who watched from the sidelines with growing unease.

When it came time to open presents, Evette's eyes sparkled with excitement as she tore into her gifts, her laughter filling the room. But Elijah's eyes remained depressed, his heart heavy with the knowledge that his father had not bothered to give him a gift for his birthday.

The guests at the party began to notice Michael's neglectful attitude toward Elijah, their whispers and sideways glances spreading like wildfire through the room. Murmurs of concern mingled with judgmental stares, as the once harmonious atmosphere soured with the weight of unspoken accusations.

As I stood in the middle of the family living room, my heart was heavy with sorrow. I watched helplessly as the tension escalated, my attempts to mediate and bring calm seemingly unnoticed.

Michael's temper flared, his words sharp and his attention dismissive, causing visible pain and confusion in Elijah's young eyes. The more I tried to intervene, to explain or soothe the growing discord, the more it seemed my words evaporated into thin air, unheard and unheeded.

Caught up in his frustrations, Michael seemed completely oblivious to the emotional turmoil swirling around him. He failed to see the hurt reflected in Elijah's face or the way Elijah's shoulders slumped, weighed down by disappointment and misunderstanding. Nor did he notice the way my voice cracked with emotional strain as I reached out to him, trying to bridge the gap that was widening between him and our son.

This ongoing struggle was not just about the moments of tension but about the profound rift it was creating within our family. I felt each harsh word and every cold dismissal deeply, not only as a mother but as a partner struggling to maintain harmony in our household. The home that should have been a sanctuary of love and understanding was turning into a battleground of words and cold shoulders.

My heart ached not just for the present pain but for the future implications of these conflicts. I feared the lasting impact they might have on Elijah, who was sensitive and observant, always looking to his parents for reassurance and love. Each unresolved conflict, each moment of disregard from Michael, was like a small crack in the foundation of Elijah's security and self-esteem.

Despite the pain and frustration, I did not give up. I knew I had to keep trying to heal the rifts and bring understanding and compassion back into our family. My love for my children and my commitment to their well-being kept me determined to find a way through the tension, to reach Michael, and to restore the warmth and unity that had once defined our family.

As the party drew to a close, my smile faltered, a bittersweet reminder of the challenges ahead. Though the day had been filled with laughter and joy, the shadow of Michael's neglect hung heavy in the air, casting a sadness over the celebration.

FOUR

As the days turned into weeks and the weeks became months, I felt the walls of our home begin to close in on me. I felt trapped and alone. This wasn't a peaceful loneliness but a deep, haunting loneliness. The air was thick with unspoken words and unresolved tensions, like a fog clouding my mind and making me sad. Michael, who once made me feel safe and warm, had grown cold and distant, especially toward Elijah. Elijah's special needs seemed to push them further apart.

Every day, I noticed Michael caring less and less about Elijah. This unspoken rejection hurt me deeply, but I refused to let it define Elijah's life. My love for Elijah was fierce and protective, a bright light against the darkness of Michael's neglect. I clung to hope and became even more determined. To me, Elijah was not a burden but a testament to pure love's endurance. His every smile was a victory over his challenges. I vowed to protect my children from the pain of indifference and promised myself I would fight for Elijah's right to be loved and accepted by his father.

One evening, when it was getting dark and the room was filled with long shadows, I saw Michael by himself, staring at the TV without really paying attention. The sound from the TV seemed far away, more like a soft whisper compared to how loud my heart was pounding in my chest. I felt nervous but also determined and I decided to go into the room anyway.

"Elijah needs you," I began, my voice trembling.

"He's not just a set of challenges, Michael—he's your son. He laughs, he loves, and he brings joy into our lives in ways no one else could." My words were full of emotion as I pleaded for Michael to see the son I loved beyond his disabilities.

"Can't you see his strength? His resilience? Please, just look at him, really look at him, and see what I see." But Michael's face remained blank, his eyes cold.

"You're imagining things, Evelyn," he said sharply, his voice full of scorn.

"You see what you want to see because it makes you feel better. But I'm living in the real world."

Michael's disregard for my feelings and Elijah's well-being hurt more than any physical wound could. This heartless dismissal was the final straw.

"How can you be so cold?" I cried out, my frustration turning into anger.

"You're his father! He deserves your love, not your neglectfulness!"

Michael scoffed and turned away, and that finally broke my last bit of control. In a burst of strong emotion, I slapped Michael across the face. The sound echoed through the room like thunder. I was just as shocked by what I had done as Michael looked.

"I want a divorce," I said, my voice trembling with a mix of anger and determination.

"I can't do this anymore. Not with someone who refuses to love his own child."

The fight that followed was intense, full of built-up emotions and harsh words. Michael's anger flared as he shouted, putting up defenses like iron gates. I was fueled by years of frustration and heartache and stood my ground, with each word being a promise to fight for a better life for Elijah.

After our fiery argument, the house that once felt warm and full of family life now felt cold and empty. That night, as the shadows grew long and the world outside our windows whispered of midnight, I made a decision that widened the gap between us. I told Michael to take his pillow and blanket and sleep on the couch. The master bedroom, once our shared space, was now mine alone, off-limits to him as if to protect me from more pain.

Michael moved without arguing, a sullen figure retreating into the dim light of the living room. The sound of the couch springs creaking under his weight seemed to punctuate the finality of my decision. Alone in the bedroom, I sat on the edge of our bed, a mix of emotions running through me. The room felt too large and too quiet, filled only with the echoes of what used to be.

In the quiet hours of the night, I wrestled with a storm of feelings. There was relief, at first, cold and hard—relief that I had finally said the words, that I had drawn a line. But soon, darker emotions seeped through. There was the anger I had with myself for the years of excuses I had made for Michael; for the way I had allowed hope to keep me in a false sense of family harmony.

And then there was fear—fear of the unknown, of the future I had to face alone, and of the legal and emotional battles that lay ahead. How would I manage it all? The thought of going to the courthouse to file for divorce felt overwhelming in the quiet darkness, each thought a weight added to my already heavy burden.

But perhaps what weighed on me the most was the guilt—sharp and relentless. I scolded myself for staying in the marriage for so long, for allowing what was meant to be love to become mere indifference. This guilt chewed at me relentlessly, bringing with it the dreadful thought that my hesitation might one day lead Elijah to not only resent Michael but me as well. What if my son came to believe that the cold, neglectful environment he was growing up in was all that he deserved? The fear that my choices might have indirectly harmed his emotional well-being haunted me, an unrelenting shadow that refused to be silenced.

In the days that followed, while Michael sat in silent withdrawal on the couch, I began to make my plans. Each step was measured and heavy, carrying both the weight of my newfound resolve and the chains of past regrets. I knew I had to move forward, not just for my own sake but for Elijah's as well. It was crucial to show him what it meant to stand up for oneself, to choose a path filled with respect and love, rather than to settle for a mere shadow of what life could offer.

During those days, I was being tested. It made me more determined and helped me focus on the future I wanted to create. As I made lists, scheduled appointments, and prepared the necessary documents, each task marked a step away from my past and a step toward reclaiming my life. The nights were long and full of thinking, but each morning brought a new sense of purpose.

As the weight of my choices settled on me, I found myself dealing with a mix of emotions, especially a deep feeling of guilt. This feeling became particularly strong when I thought about the impact of the divorce on Evette. Unlike Elijah, she had formed a different kind of bond with Michael. Despite his failings with her brother, Michael had been a more present and engaged father to Evette, and the thought of breaking that relationship pained me deeply.

On a quiet evening, after the kids had gone to bed, I sat alone in the dim light of the living room, with a cup of tea cooling that was untouched on the coffee table in front of me. The silence of the house seemed to amplify my inner turmoil. I thought about the future, imagining the different paths my life might take once the divorce was finalized, each scenario tinged with the bitter taste of guilt.

My thoughts drifted to the day I would have to tell Evette about the divorce. How would I explain that our family was about to change forever? How could I justify taking her away from her father when he had shown nothing but love and attentiveness towards her? The guilt was a gnawing presence, eating away at the resolve I had felt earlier. I worried about the long-term effects on Evette and the potential resentment and confusion that might arise from this upheaval.

I weighed my options, my mind racing through possible outcomes. Could there be a way to ensure Michael remained a significant part of Evette's life? The idea of shared custody came to mind, but it brought with it a surge of anxiety—how would Elijah handle the back-and-forth between two homes, especially with his specific needs and the routines so vital to his sense of security?

The weight of my decision felt heavy. Was I being selfish by choosing a separation that might be better for me and Elijah but could hurt Evette? My heart ached at the thought of my daughter having to grow up in a divided home, her childhood memories split between two different lives.

Needing some comfort or advice, I reached for my phone to call Emma, my sister. But as my fingers hovered over her contact, I hesitated. It was late, and my pride held me back. Instead, I turned to my journal, pouring out my fears and doubts onto the pages in a silent talk with myself. Writing brought temporary relief, helping me sort through my thoughts and face my emotions.

As the night went on, I knew that writing couldn't fully ease my guilt or give me all the answers. Yet, it gave me a moment of clarity, reminding me that this journey wasn't just about escaping a failing marriage, but about finding a healthier, happier life for all my children, despite the challenges ahead.

I woke up early, while it was still dark outside. Before I could prepare for the day, I had an important task—to make sure Elijah was well cared for. Quietly, I entered his room, where he lay sleeping peacefully, unaware of the important day ahead.

Gently, I woke Elijah, easing him out of sleep with soft words and the promise of his usual breakfast. Dressing him took patience and careful attention, as he needed help with his clothes and shoes—tasks that Michael, in his current state of neglect, might have easily overlooked.

Once Elijah was ready and had his breakfast, I packed a small bag with things he might need—some snacks, his favorite toy to keep him calm, and a few books. As we walked out the door, I felt more determined than ever, not just for me, but for Elijah. He needed me to be strong today.

Driving to the courthouse, my hands were steady on the wheel, but inside, I felt both scared and determined. The courthouse looked big and serious, making it clear that big changes were coming.

I took a deep breath and opened the big doors, holding Elijah's hand tightly. The cool air inside gave me a little boost of courage. As we waited to file the divorce papers, all sorts of memories came flooding back—some good, some bad. Each one made me even more sure that I needed to do this, not just for my peace of mind but for my son's future too.

Inside, I talked with a lawyer, a kind and straightforward woman who explained what would happen in the next few months. We talked about how to handle custody for Elijah, considering his needs, and what the financial side of things would look like after the split. The lawyer helped me understand all the paperwork and legal terms, making everything seem less overwhelming.

When we got home, I sat down with Evette and Elijah and explained the changes that were coming. I made sure to fill our talk with love. It was a tender moment as I reassured them that even though some things would change, my love for them would always stay the same. I answered their questions as best as I could, feeling sad about their confusion and curiosity.

That night, after the house was quiet, I took some time to think. I thought about everything that had happened, feeling horrible about the thought of my marriage ending but, I was also a bit hopeful about what was ahead. I wrote down my thoughts and fears, making plans not just for tomorrow but for the life I wanted to rebuild. This quiet time helped me see that I could make a new start, not just get by but truly thrive.

The next rose the next morning and while I was making breakfast, we had a surprise visit from my sister Emma. Emma didn't just offer emotional support but also helped with practical things. We spent the evening making plans, sharing laughs, and even shedding some tears, reminding me that I don't have to go through tough times alone. Emma's visit showed me the strength that comes from having support from people you love.

FIVE

I tried to keep things normal for the kids, even though inside, I was counting each day with anxious anticipation. My interactions with Michael were limited to what was necessary, as I tried to protect both myself and the children from extra stress. During this time, I focused on our daily routines, keeping the children engaged and happy while quietly dealing with my moments of worry and hope when they weren't looking.

While waiting for changes to unfold, I wasn't just sitting around. I started preparing for our new life. This included searching for a new home in a welcoming neighborhood, and looking up schools and support options for Elijah. I also had to consider job opportunities or ways to grow my interests and skills. These tasks helped distract me from my current stress and were steps toward building our future.

Emma's arrival at my house brought comfort and familiarity. As soon as she walked in, we locked eyes, and without a word, moved towards each other for a long, heartfelt hug. This embrace was more than a simple greeting; it was full of love, support, and understanding. In that quiet moment, years of memories and shared understanding flowed between us, strengthening our bond and giving mutual comfort amidst the challenges of life.

After enjoying our reunion, we turned our attention to the children, who were excited to share their day's stories with their aunt. With smiles and laughter, Emma greeted each child, her presence bringing extra joy to our home. Together, we settled the kids in the living room with snacks—bowls of popcorn and some sliced fruit—and started a family-friendly movie. The kids' excitement was clear as they arranged themselves on the couch, quickly engrossed in the movie.

With the children happily occupied, Emma and I took the chance to slip into the kitchen for a more private talk. We each grabbed a cup of coffee, the familiar ritual easing us into comfort. Sitting at the kitchen table, facing each other, we were ready to dive into deeper conversations. This was our time to share not just the good things in our lives but also the worries and challenges that we often kept to ourselves.

In the comfort of my kitchen, Emma and I spoke openly and honestly. We talked about our hopes, our worries, and the everyday little things. I shared my concerns about finding the right home and making sure it met all of Elijah's needs. Emma listened and gave thoughtful advice, always ready to help me figure things out. This heart-to-heart was a tradition for us, one that strengthened our sisterly bond and our commitment to support each other through whatever life might bring.

"Tell me everything, Ev," Emma urged gently, her eyes showing her worry. I took a deep breath, my heart heavy with all I had been through but relieved to finally share my burdens. As I told her about the recent events—the arguments, my decision to file for divorce, and the waiting—Emma listened intently, her face showing surprise, sadness, and then a firm understanding.

As I shared the weight of my struggles and the daunting task of finding a suitable home, Emma listened closely. She saw the stress in my tired eyes and the weariness in how I carried myself. During our heartfelt talk, Emma seemed to genuinely understand how hard things had been for me.

Wanting to help, Emma leaned forward, her face showing determined compassion.

"Why don't you move closer to me?" she suggested, her voice full of hope and sincerity.

"You and the kids need a fresh start, something new and positive. And I want to be there for you, not just sometimes or over the phone, but really there, where you need me."

Her offer was heartfelt, coming from a place of true love and the desire to give real support. Emma imagined a life where she could be more involved, where spontaneous visits, shared dinners, and regular family gatherings were normal. She saw how this could help me and the kids rebuild and refresh our lives with her nearby to support us whenever we needed it.

"This could be a good change for all of us," Emma continued, reaching out to hold my hand, showing her commitment.

"Being neighbors, helping each other out more, watching the kids grow up together—it's something I think could really work for us."

Her words filled the air, full of potential and promise, offering me not just a new place to live, but the reassurance of having my sister's steadfast support just a stone's throw away. It was a proposal that touched the heart of our bond, a chance to strengthen our sisterhood and make sure that the children and I would not have to face any of life's challenges alone anymore.

Emma went on to describe how she could help, saying,

"You'll have someone to help with the kids, to pick them up from school if you need, or just to have dinner ready when you're overwhelmed." She talked about the community, the schools, and even potential job opportunities for me in her city. Her enthusiasm was infectious, and she covered practical points while emphasizing the emotional benefits of being surrounded by family.

I was touched and moved by her offer. The thought of moving to a new city and state was daunting, but the idea of having Emma close and a supportive family network gave me hope. Emma's presence would not only lighten the logistical and emotional load but also provide a stable, loving environment for the kids as they dealt with the changes. However, the decision also involved the children's well-being, especially Evette's. Understanding this, Emma suggested we talk directly to Evette about the move, to involve her in the decision-making process and consider her feelings.

Later, with gentle encouragement from both Emma and me, Evette listened to the idea of moving closer to her aunt. Emma engaged her warmly, highlighting how fun it would be to have her nearby and the new places they could explore together. Evette's initial hesitation turned into curiosity as she thought about the possibilities of new adventures and being part of a close-knit family circle.

In the middle of talking to Evette about the move, a big moment came with a simple phone call. My lawyer told me that the divorce was final. My lawyer told me that Michael didn't fight for anything, not even the kids, or the thought of us leaving and moving to California. The news from the lawyer brought relief, followed by a strong feeling of empowerment and closure. It was a moment of deep change, marked by tears of relief and smiles of hope.

Feeling strong from this legal closure, and grateful that it was not a long drawn-out process, I started the real steps of moving forward. It was a big moment, filled with both the excitement of new beginnings and the sad feelings of leaving familiar places behind. As I prepared to move out, I sat down with the kids and gently explained that we were about to start a new chapter in our lives.

"This is going to be a fresh start for us, a new adventure," I told them, my voice steady but full of hope. The children looked at me, their faces showing a mix of curiosity and uncertainty. They could feel how important this change was.

As we started packing up the things in our home, each room reminded us of the journey we had been on. Boxes stacked up, each filled with pieces of our past—books, toys, dishes—all getting ready for our new place. Packing was both a symbol and a practical step, marking our move from what had once been our safe place.

I led the packing with calm efficiency, but I could feel the emotions bubbling beneath the surface. The kids had lots of questions and worries about what was coming.

"Will we make new friends? What will our new school be like?" Evette asked. I answered each question with calm reassurance, promising them both stability and continuity.

"We're going to have a wonderful home," I assured them.

"You'll each get your own new rooms to decorate. We'll explore parks, libraries, and find the best ice cream spots." My words painted a picture of a future that was safe and full of chances for happiness and exploration.

Throughout the packing and planning, I stayed strong and reassuring for my children, easing their worries with my optimism. I promised them that no matter where we were, our love for each other would never change. This move was just about finding a new place to continue our story, a place where we could make new memories while keeping the love and stability that had always been the core of our family.

As we drove away from our old home, I took one last look in the rearview mirror, a symbolic farewell to what we were leaving behind. Ahead was our new home, waiting to be filled with new memories, free from the past shadows.

After saying goodbye to our old place, we drove to Emma's house, which would be our temporary home while I looked for the perfect new place. Pulling into Emma's driveway and seeing her waiting with open arms was a powerful reminder of the support system we had.

Emma helped us unload and settle in. Her home was warm and inviting. She showed the kids their rooms, which she had already set up just for them. Evette's room was bright and cheerful, decorated with posters of her favorite cartoons, and Elijah's was quiet, comfortable, and filled with the sensory toys he loved.

For me, the transition was bittersweet. I was relieved to have a safe place for my kids, but living in someone else's home had its challenges. I felt dependent and unsure about the future. That night, as the house quieted down, Emma and I sat down with our tea, discussing my house-hunting plans. Emma reassured me, listing concrete ways she would help, like joining me to check houses for accessibility features for Elijah.

Over the next few days, we started settling into a routine at Emma's house. The kids adapted well, comforted by their aunt's presence. Emma actively helped me navigate this new phase, arranging playdates for Evette and joining Elijah at therapy sessions nearby. This support allowed me to focus on finding a house and deepened the bond between Emma and the children.

I approached the search for a new home with a meticulous eye, prioritizing Elijah's needs but also looking for a place that felt right for us all. I knew every detail mattered—the layout of the rooms, no stairs, good schools nearby, and a friendly neighborhood. My list was long and detailed, reflecting my commitment to my family's well-being.

As I delved into the real estate market, I quickly ran into the same challenges many homebuyers face. Properties that looked perfect online often didn't live up to the promise in person. Pictures showed bright, airy rooms and big backyards, but the reality was often cramped rooms and neglected gardens. Each visit added to my stress and disappointment, making the hunt for a home increasingly frustrating.

Moreover, finding a house that was wheelchair accessible for Elijah and in a good neighborhood was tough. The few places that did meet Elijah's needs were often in less-than-ideal locations or were way over our budget. It was rare to find a house that had everything—accessibility, affordability, and a welcoming community—making the search both exhausting and disheartening.

Despite these obstacles, I stayed determined. I was set on finding the perfect house—one that would support Elijah's independence and provide a safe, loving environment for us all. I went to see countless properties, asked loads of questions, and spent nights looking over listings and planning visits for the next day.

The journey through the real estate market tested my patience. With every setback, I had to gather my strength all over again, reminded of how important it was to find the right place for my family's needs and the dreams I had for our future together. I was meticulous and had strict criteria, which helped me get through the complications of house hunting and towards finding a place we could truly call home.

One evening, after a day of looking at houses that didn't work for us, I felt frustrated and scared for the future. So, I talked to Emma about it. We sat in her kitchen, with the aroma of the chamomile tea brewing on the stove. The soft glow of the sunset shining through the window made everything feel cozy. I told Emma all of the things that were worrying me, and she listened carefully, which helped me calm down.

"I don't know if we'll ever find the right place," I confessed, my voice trembling with the strain of my worries.

"Every house we see seems to have something wrong with it. I just want a safe, welcoming home for the kids, where Elijah can move around freely, and where we can all start fresh."

Emma reached across the table and took my hand in hers, her touch warm and reassuring. Her eyes, filled with understanding and compassion, met mine.

"I know this has been incredibly hard, Ev," she said softly.

"But I truly believe that the right home is out there for you. Sometimes, it just takes a bit longer to find something that meets all our needs. You've been so strong and determined, and that's going to pay off."

She gave my hand a gentle squeeze, her smile radiating encouragement.

"Remember, you're not alone in this. We're in this together. And no matter how long it takes, you and the kids have a home here with me. You don't have to rush or settle for anything less than perfect. Take your time. Use this as an opportunity to really find a place that feels like home."

What she said made me feel better when I was feeling tired and upset. I felt the tension in my shoulders ease as her reassurances sank in. Emma continued,

"Think of this as a journey, not just a destination. Every step you take, every house you visit, is bringing you closer to that perfect home. And in the meantime, you have a safe, loving place here. The kids are happy, and we're making new memories every day."

Emma's encouragement lit a spark of hope within me. Her unwavering support and belief in our journey renewed my resolve. I realized that while the search was challenging, it was also a testament to my commitment to my children's future. With Emma by my side, I knew I could face the setbacks and keep moving forward.

At that moment, sitting in Emma's kitchen, I felt very grateful for my sister's support, for the temporary haven she provided, and for the strength I found within myself to keep going. Emma's words wrapped around me like a comforting blanket, reminding me that every step of this journey was leading us to a better place.

As I went to bed that night, I found myself in what seemed like a hole that I mentally and emotionally couldn't get myself out of. I quietly cried for hours. I tried to act like things weren't as bad as they were but at that moment I felt like I was emotionally out of control. That was when Emma softly knocked on the door of her guest room. I quickly wiped my eyes and prepared for her to come in and ask me what was going on. When she did, I let it all out.

Life after the divorce with Michael had been an uphill battle, a relentless struggle that seemed to have no end in sight. Each day felt like a marathon, with hurdles and obstacles at every turn. Taking care of Evette and Elijah on my own was like trying to juggle a dozen balls at once, and sometimes, inevitably, a few would slip through my fingers. There were moments when it felt like I was drowning in a sea of responsibilities, each one pressing down on me like a weight on my chest, making it hard to catch my breath.

Evette and Elijah are my whole world, the center of my universe, and their well-being is my top priority. But despite my love for them, there are moments when the challenges of single parenthood feel overwhelming. Elijah's special needs add an extra layer of complexity to our daily lives. Simple tasks that others take for granted become monumental feats for us. Finding a job that can accommodate his unique requirements seems like searching for a needle in a haystack. And the constant worry about finding a home that's not just suitable but fully accessible for him adds another layer of stress to my already overflowing plate. Every day feels like a battle against the odds, with uncertainty looming on the horizon, but I refuse to let it break me.

I'm grateful for my sister, Emma. She's been my constant support through this tough time. When things got really hard, she was there to hold me up. It was Emma who told me I should talk to someone professional about all the feelings I've been dealing with. At first, I wasn't sure about talking to someone I didn't know, but Emma kept cheering me on. She said it's perfectly okay to ask for help when you're struggling, and she was right.

After thinking about it for a while, I made up my mind to try counseling. I searched online and found a therapist called Dr. Sarah Johnson. Something about her profile clicked with me, so I decided to book an appointment with her. As I continued to scroll through Dr. Johnson's profile, I noticed that she specialized in family therapy and cognitive behavioral therapy (CBT), which sounded like exactly what I needed. Her description talked about creating a safe and supportive space for clients to explore their emotions and find solutions to their problems, which truly resonated with me. Additionally, her warm smile in the profile picture gave me a sense of comfort and reassurance. Overall, it just felt like she could understand what I was going through and help me navigate through it.

The first session with Dr. Johnson was held in her office with soft lighting and a comfortable loveseat. Despite the inviting atmosphere, I still felt a knot of nervousness in my stomach as I sat down and began to open up about my struggles. Talking about the events leading to the divorce and the challenges of single motherhood made me feel incredibly vulnerable like I was laying bare all my innermost thoughts and emotions.

However, Dr. Johnson's demeanor immediately put me at ease. She sat across from me with a gentle expression, leaning forward slightly as she listened intently to every word I said. Her body language conveyed a sense of empathy and understanding, which helped me feel validated and heard. Whenever I paused or hesitated, she would nod encouragingly, prompting me to continue sharing my thoughts and feelings.

Throughout the session, Dr. Johnson's patience and attentiveness never wavered. She asked insightful questions and offered supportive comments, creating a safe space for me to explore my emotions without fear of judgment. Her genuine interest in my story and her willingness to listen without interrupting made me feel valued and respected, easing my anxiety and allowing me to open up more freely.

In the weeks that followed, I kept going to therapy with Dr. Johnson. She helped me untangle all the emotions that were weighing me down, using techniques like talk therapy and CBT. She encouraged me to challenge the negative thoughts and beliefs that were holding me back, especially the ones that made me blame myself for everything that had happened with Michael and Elijah.

As the weeks passed, I began to feel something shifting inside me. It was like a heavy weight was lifted off my shoulders. The guilt and self-blame that had been dragging me down slowly started to fade away. Instead of being so hard on myself, I started to treat myself with kindness and understanding, like I would a good friend. I realized that everyone makes mistakes, including me, and that it's okay to forgive myself and move forward. With Dr. Johnson's help, I started to focus more on the future, thinking about all the positive changes I wanted to make for myself and my children.

After going to therapy for four months, I noticed a change in myself. I felt like a weight had been lifted off my shoulders. I was more sure of myself and more optimistic about the future than I had been in a while. The hurtful things from before were still there, but they didn't control me like they used to. With Dr. Johnson's guidance, I started to heal and learn more about myself, and I knew that even after therapy ended, my journey to feeling better would keep going.

SIX

The morning began with soft sunlight shining through the sheer curtains in Emma's guest room. It was a quiet Saturday, the kind of day that felt like something good might happen. Outside, the sky was clear and blue, without a single cloud, promising a day without rain.

I quietly got out of bed, trying not to wake the twins or Emma, who had been up late working on her lesson plans. The air outside was cool but hinted at a warm afternoon. I took a deep breath, enjoying the fresh air and the smell of blooming flowers.

I walked to my car, parked under an old oak tree in Emma's yard. The leaves rustled softly above me. I unlocked the car, put my coffee in the cup holder, and placed a small stack of house listings on the passenger seat. Today, I felt hopeful—maybe today I would find the perfect place for me and the twins.

I started the car and pulled away from the curb, the gravel crunching under the tires. The neighborhood was waking up; joggers nodded hello as they passed by, and birds were singing cheerfully in the trees. The sun was rising higher, casting a golden glow over the houses on the quiet street.

I turned on the radio to a soft music station, letting the calm tunes fill the car as I drove to the first address on my list. The day was full of possibilities, and I was ready for whatever came my way.

Driving through town, I felt both excited and nervous. I soon arrived at the house. The yard was messy, with a dirty pond and tall grass. The house looked old and run-down, with peeling paint and dusty windows.

I tried to stay positive as I met Janet, the realtor, who greeted me with a smile. We went inside, but my hopes fell right away. The entrance was small, leading to dark, cramped rooms. The kitchen was old and tiny. As I walked through the house, my disappointment grew. The hallways were too narrow, and the rooms were too small for Elijah's wheelchair and equipment.

Even though I was let down, I reminded myself that this was just one house. The day was still young, and there were other places to see. I thanked Janet and went back to my car, ready to move on to the next listing. The search for our new home continued, and with each house, I learned more about what we needed and what we could compromise on.

As I drove away from the disappointing house, I took another deep breath, letting the fresh air fill my lungs again. The sun was shining brighter, and the day still held promise. I knew finding the right home would take time and patience, but I was determined to keep looking until I found the perfect place for us.

I made up my mind quickly and thanked Janet, explaining that the house wasn't accessible enough for my son. Janet understood and promised to keep looking for a better fit. As I drove away, I felt a mix of frustration and hope. Finding the right home was hard, but I had to keep trying for my family.

After leaving the house, I drove aimlessly for a while, my thoughts clouded with worry. Every house seemed too small or too far from what we needed. My heart grew heavier with each passing minute. Just as I was about to call it a day, my phone rang.

It was Janet, her voice upbeat.

"Evelyn, you might want to see this," she said excitedly.

"A colleague of mine just listed a house that could be perfect. It's a bit outside of town, about 20 minutes away. I really think you need to see it for yourself."

Her hopeful tone sparked a little flame of optimism in me. I quickly agreed to head over.

"I'll be there as soon as I can," I responded, feeling a new purpose.

As I set the GPS and started toward the new location, I felt a mix of nervousness and excitement. The possibility of finding a house that could truly be a home for my family lifted my spirits. I allowed myself to feel a bit of hope, my mind daring to imagine a place where my children could thrive and where we could start anew. The drive felt shorter than it was, my anticipation building with each mile.

I turned up the music, letting the upbeat tunes fill the car, mirroring the hopeful rhythm of my thoughts. As I neared the address Janet had given me, my grip on the steering wheel tightened—a good sign, I told myself. Maybe, just maybe, this could be the one.

As I turned onto the street where the new house was located, my heart pounded with a mix of excitement and cautious hope. The neighborhood was pleasantly quiet, with homes spaced just right—not too close to feel crowded, yet not too far to feel isolated. It was the kind of balance I had been hoping to find, a place where my kids could have space yet still feel part of a community.

When I pulled up to the address, my eyes widened in surprise and delight. The house stood proudly on a well-kept lawn, framed by mature trees that whispered of age and stability. The yard was large enough for my children to play freely but not so big as to demand excessive upkeep. A gentle slope led up to a welcoming front porch adorned with hanging planters, their blooms adding splashes of color.

The exterior of the house was painted a soft, cheerful yellow, glowing in the morning light. It looked so inviting, a stark contrast to the homes I had seen earlier. The windows were large, promising plenty of natural light inside, and the path to the front door was bordered with small shrubs and flowers, all neatly trimmed.

As I stepped out of the car and walked toward the house, I began to feel more excited. Janet greeted me with a warm smile and led me inside. The moment I walked through the door, I was met with an airy, bright space that felt immediately welcoming. The living room was spacious, with wide windows letting in streams of sunlight.

I could easily picture Elijah moving around freely in his wheelchair, and Evette playing happily in the open area. The kitchen was modern and roomy, with enough space for family meals and gatherings. Each room we walked through seemed to meet our needs, with wide hallways and accessible spaces that would make daily life easier for Elijah.

I felt relief and excitement. The house felt right. As Janet showed me around, I could see our future unfolding here—a place where we could all feel safe, happy, and at home. It was more than just a house; it felt like the start of a new chapter for our family.

Stepping out of my car, I felt a gentle breeze that carried the faint scent of lilacs. I could hear children playing somewhere nearby. It felt like a neighborhood where life was lived joyfully and openly. My heart felt lighter than it had in days, and I felt a flutter of excitement rising in my chest.

I stood for a moment, taking it all in, imagining my family here—the laughter of my children playing in the yard, afternoons spent on that inviting porch, peaceful evenings under the shade of those trees. It felt right, almost like a dream I had not fully imagined until now.

Filled with hope, I walked up the path to meet Janet, who was waiting at the front door with a knowing smile, as if she too could tell that this house might just be the one. We walked up the paved driveway together. My eyes traced the lines of the ranch-style home. The house was painted a dignified dark gray, with crisp white trim around the windows and doors, giving it a classic, timeless look. The driveway led to a spacious two-car garage, suggesting practicality and convenience.

The abundance of windows caught my attention next. They were large and looked new, promising not only great views of the surrounding yard but also plenty of natural light inside. I appreciated the thought of sunlight filling the rooms, imagining how it would make the house feel warm and welcoming.

As we approached, the simplicity and horizontal layout of the ranch design appealed to my practical side. It meant fewer stairs to navigate, which would make it easier for Elijah to move around in his wheelchair. The front yard continued around the side of the house to a backyard that was visible from the driveway, showing more space that seemed perfect for my children to play and explore safely.

Janet opened the front door, and we stepped inside. Immediately, I was struck by the open feel of the living area. The living room flowed into the dining space, with only a few steps leading to the kitchen that added a touch of character without compromising accessibility. The open floor plan seemed ideal for keeping an eye on the kids and for family gatherings.

"Most of the living spaces are on this side of the house," Janet explained as we moved through the house, pointing out the smart layout.

"It's perfect for someone who needs easy access throughout the home."

Each room we entered maintained the promise shown outside—spacious, with thoughtful touches like wide doorways and minimal thresholds, which would make mobility easier for Elijah. The kitchen was modern with updated appliances and plenty of counter space, ideal for me as I enjoyed cooking with the kids.

As we toured, I began to feel more attached to the house. It wasn't just the physical aspects but the potential it represented—a safe, beautiful, and functional space where my family could thrive.

Continuing the tour, my appreciation for the thoughtful details grew. Janet led me to the laundry room, conveniently located on the main level, just off the kitchen. I nodded approvingly, recognizing how much easier this would make daily chores, especially with no stairs to contend with. The practicality of its location meant I could multitask efficiently, keeping an eye on meals in the kitchen while handling laundry.

Next, we walked down a short hallway to inspect the bedrooms. The hallway was wide enough for Elijah to move through without having to worry about bumping into the walls. The first two bedrooms were directly across from a large bathroom, an arrangement I found ideal. It meant that the twins could easily access the bathroom at night, and I could quickly assist them if needed. I peeked inside the bathroom and was pleasantly surprised by its size and design. The bathtub was custom-made, and slightly raised to reduce the strain on my back when helping Elijah during bath times. The room also featured grab bars and a wide, flat floor, which would allow for easy movement of Elijah's gait trainer.

The master bedroom was just a few steps down the hall, close enough to the children's rooms to give me peace of mind but still offering a bit of privacy. I stepped inside and felt a wave of relief at the spacious layout, which promised restful nights and quiet moments away from the household bustle.

I couldn't help but express my thoughts aloud.

"I love how everything is arranged just right," I said to Janet, my voice filled with hopeful tones.

"It's like this house was made for us." Janet smiled, pleased with my reaction.

"It's wonderful when a house feels like a home right away," she replied.

As we finished the tour, I had a feeling of contentment that I hadn't experienced when I viewed any of the other houses. Each feature seemed designed with my family's needs in mind, from the accessible bathroom to the practicality of the laundry room. I could already envision my family living here, each space filled with laughter and life.

Just before the tour ended we took a walk through the backyard. It offered a fenced-in backyard and plenty of room for the kids to play. I stood there thinking, I knew this house could be our new beginning. It wasn't just a building; it was a potential home where my family could grow and thrive.

My excitement surged as I finished touring the house, already picturing my family settling into each room. Turning to Janet, I took a deep breath and said,

"I want this house. Let's make an offer." The words were out before I even thought to ask about the price. As my excitement momentarily gave way to anxiety, I braced myself for the possibility that the house might be out of my reach financially.

"What's the asking price?" I asked, my voice tinged with nervous anticipation.

Janet flipped through her papers, and then looked up with an expression of disbelief.

"You won't believe this, Evelyn. This house is listed at $150,000." My eyes widened in shock.

"Really? But how? The houses around here go for so much more," I stammered, hardly daring to believe my luck. Janet nodded, equally astonished.

"It's true. It's a one-of-a-kind situation. The owners are moving overseas and are looking for a quick sale. They want to pass the house to someone who'll appreciate it. It seems like it's meant to be." I thought to myself how I could pay for the house with the money I had sitting in my bank account from our house in Florida.

For a four-bedroom house with two bathrooms, a fenced backyard, and a sunroom that could be used as a therapy room for Elijah, the price was incredibly low. Most homes in the neighborhood were listed for double or even triple that amount. I felt a rush of gratitude wash over me. I had prayed for the right home to come along, one where my children could thrive and grow, and it seemed my prayers had been answered.

With a heart full of hope and a smile brimming with joy, I looked at Janet.

"Let's do this. I don't want to lose this opportunity." Janet's smile matched my enthusiasm as she replied,

"I'll get the paperwork started right away."

As we stepped outside, I took a moment to look back at the house. It wasn't just the features or the price that had stolen my heart; it was the feeling of rightness that enveloped me the moment I walked in. I knew that if I kept faith, everything would fall into place. And today, it felt like everything indeed was.

SEVEN

After deciding to make an offer on the house, I drove home, filled with a mix of nervous excitement and bubbling joy. The drive seemed shorter than usual, my mind replaying every detail of the house that could soon become my family's new home. Pulling into Emma's driveway, I saw my children playing in the yard, their laughter a sweet melody that lifted my spirits even higher.

Stepping out of the car, my smile was wide with the good news I carried. I gathered my children around, ushering them inside with an eagerness that piqued their curiosity. Emma noticed the unusual sparkle in my eyes and followed us into the living room, sensing that I had something important to share.

Once inside, I gathered everyone on the comfortable, well-worn couch. The children's eyes were wide with anticipation, and Emma looked on, a supportive smile gracing her lips.

"I had quite the day," I began, my voice tinged with excitement.

"I saw a house today—not just any house, but I think... I think it might be the one." I let the significance of my words settle on each of them.

"The house is beautiful, spacious, and sunny, with a big yard for you all to play in," I continued, turning to my children with a softness in my eyes.

"And guess what? It has a room that could be perfect for therapy sessions, and it's all on one level, so it's easy for everyone to get around."

The kids exchanged looks of cautious excitement, their expressions reflecting a mix of hope and the fear of disappointment. I reached out, squeezing their hands gently.

"I made an offer on it. If all goes well, that might be our new home." Emma, always the supportive sister, leaned in closer.

"That's wonderful, Evie! This sounds like a fresh start for you all. How do you feel?"

"I'm a bit nervous," I admitted, my gaze flicking to each face, seeking reassurance.

"But when I walked through that house, it felt right. It felt like... home." My voice was steady, imbued with a quiet strength that came from my deep-rooted hope.

The children, sensing my optimism, began to ask questions about their potential new bedrooms and the yard, their voices bubbling with excitement. Emma watched the scene, her heart full, knowing the struggles I had faced and feeling a profound relief that I might finally find the peace and stability we so deserved.

We spent the rest of the evening discussing potential room arrangements and decorating ideas, the house filling with renewed hope and anticipation. For me, sharing this moment with my family, seeing their smiles, and hearing their laughter, reinforced my belief that I had made the right decision.

Three days after I shared the exciting news of a possible new home with my family, my usual morning routine was interrupted by my phone ringing. I glanced at the caller ID and saw it was Janet, my realtor. My heart skipped a beat as I quickly answered, hoping for good news.

"Evelyn, I have wonderful news," Janet said, her voice bubbling with excitement.

"Your offer on the house has been accepted! The sellers were really impressed with how quickly you moved and your clear desire for the home."

My breath caught in my throat, a mix of relief and joy washing over me.

"Really? That's amazing! I can't believe it!" I exclaimed, a broad smile spreading across my face.

"Yes, it's all set," Janet continued.

"We need to get the paperwork started and finalize everything. Can you come to the office to sign the documents? We have a bit of closing to do, but if everything goes smoothly, the house will officially be yours."

I felt a surge of excitement.

"Of course, I'll be there. When do I need to come in?" I asked, already mentally preparing to rearrange my day for this important step.

"Tomorrow morning would be perfect if you're available," Janet suggested.

"We'll have everything ready for your signature, and I'll walk you through all the details and what to expect next."

"That works. I'll see you tomorrow then. Thank you, Janet, for everything," I said, my voice thick with emotion. The reality of owning a new home, a place where my family could thrive and create new memories, was finally sinking in.

After hanging up, I sat for a moment in quiet reflection, feeling profound gratitude. I looked around at the home we would soon be leaving, every corner filled with memories of struggles and triumphs. Soon, we would start a new chapter.

With a fresh purpose, I got up and began my day, the news of the house lifting my spirits. I couldn't wait to tell Emma and the kids that their dream of a new home was about to become a reality. When I shared the news with Emma and the children, their reactions were a mix of excitement and disbelief. We immediately started the process of packing up our lives to move to the new home. It was a busy, somewhat chaotic time, but it was underpinned with a current of excitement and anticipation for the fresh start that awaited us.

I took charge, organizing boxes and sorting through belongings with a practical eye.

"Let's start with the non-essentials and seasonal items first," I instructed the kids, handing them markers to label the boxes. Emma helped by wrapping fragile items, her hands careful and precise as she placed dishes and glassware into boxes stuffed with packing paper.

The children, each given tasks that suited their abilities, shuffled around, filling boxes with toys, books, and clothes. The laughter and occasional bickering filled the house, a comforting soundtrack to the hard work. I smiled as I watched them, my heart swelling with pride at their enthusiasm and teamwork.

As we packed, I found myself reflecting on the memories associated with each item we wrapped and boxed. Each piece seemed to hold a story, a moment of our lives together.

"Remember this?" I would ask, holding up a faded photograph or a well-loved toy, sparking a flood of anecdotes and laughter.

Emma stood by my side, her presence a steady comfort.
"It's going to be great, Ev," she reassured me.
"This house—it's a new beginning, a chance to build something even better."

By the end of the day, the living room was filled with stacked boxes, each labeled and taped securely. The physical evidence of our impending move made everything seem more real, more immediate. I felt a mix of exhaustion and elation as I looked around. The process was daunting, yet the thought of moving into a home that promised so much possibility made all the effort worthwhile.

"We're doing it, kids," I announced, my voice strong and optimistic as I surveyed our progress.

"We're really doing it. Soon, we'll be in our new home, and it will be wonderful."

The kids cheered, their faces bright with joy and excitement, mirroring my emotions. Together, we continued packing, the work made lighter by our shared dreams of the days to come in our new house.

The next morning dawned bright and hopeful as I prepared to head to the realtor's office for the closing of my new house. Dressed smartly, my nerves tingled with a mixture of excitement and the solemnity of the occasion. Today, I would finalize the steps to become the owner of the house that promised a new chapter for my family.

Arriving at the office, I was greeted warmly by Janet, who had all the paperwork prepared and laid out neatly on a large table.

"Good morning, Evelyn! Everything is set up. We'll go through the documents together, and I'll explain everything as we go," Janet said, her voice reassuring.

Janet led me through each document, explaining the purpose of every page. First, there was the settlement statement, which detailed the financial transactions involved in the purchase, including the selling price, the fees associated with the closing, and the adjustments for taxes and utilities. I followed closely, my pen poised over the paper, ready to make my mark.

We continued through the documents, my excitement building with each signature. Janet explained each step patiently, ensuring I understood everything. It felt like the culmination of all my hopes and dreams for a better future for my family.

Finally, after what felt like hours but was just a thorough process, I signed the last document. Janet smiled warmly, congratulating me.

"Congratulations, Evelyn. You're now the proud owner of your new home."

Next, we reviewed the mortgage agreement. Janet outlined the terms of the loan, the interest rate, and the monthly payment schedule. I listened carefully, focusing on the numbers and terms to make sure I understood my obligations and rights.

After the mortgage documents, we went through the title papers, which confirmed the transfer of home ownership from the sellers to me. Janet explained how important it was for the title to be clear and free of any liens or disputes, assuring me that the property would be legally mine without any unforeseen problems.

After nearly an hour of careful review and explanation, I began signing the documents. My signature was steady despite the nervous fluttering in my stomach. Each signature brought me closer to making the house mine, and I felt relieved and proud of myself.

Finally, Janet handed me the keys to the house.

"Congratulations, Evelyn! The house is officially yours!" she exclaimed, giving me a small, shiny key ring.

I held the keys in my hand, feeling their weight and the reality they represented. I was overwhelmed with deep gratitude and a strong feeling of accomplishment.

"Thank you, Janet. I can't tell you how much this means to me and my family," I responded, my voice thick with emotion.

I couldn't help but let out a small, joyous laugh, tears of happiness welling up in my eyes. With the paperwork completed, I had a feeling of accomplishment, which was the most exciting part of my week. My new home awaited, and with it, the promise of a brighter, more secure future for my family. The journey ahead would be filled with challenges and triumphs, but I felt ready to embrace it all. I was ready to have a fresh start, to make the house a home filled with love, laughter, and the promise of wonderful memories.

I returned home, my heart light and my hands clutching the shiny new keys to our future. Emma was there, her face bright with a supportive smile, ready to help me begin the transition to our new home. Together, we loaded up the car with several boxes—bits and pieces of our lives packed neatly away, ready to be resettled in our new environment.

"This is just the start," I said, trying to keep the atmosphere positive as we worked.

Leaving the kids in Emma's capable hands, I drove to the new house, the trunk of my car filled with the promise of a fresh beginning. I began unloading the boxes, each one placed in the rooms I had already mentally assigned them to in my new home. The house was quiet, the echo of my movements a stark contrast to the laughter and noise that would soon fill it.

Just as I was setting down a box labeled 'Kitchen,' my phone rang. I answered it, still in a haze of moving-day chaos. Emma's voice came through, frantic and edged with panic.

"Evelyn, it's Elijah! He's having a seizure!"

Panic gripped my heart.

"Call an ambulance, Emma! I'm on my way back now!" I shouted into the phone, my hands shaking as I dropped the box I was holding.

I raced back to the car, my mind whirling with fear for my son. The drive back seemed to last forever, every red light a barrier between me and Elijah. As I pulled into Emma's driveway, the sight of the ambulance parked outside sent a shiver of fear through me.

I burst through the front door, my eyes immediately finding Elijah on the living room floor, convulsing. Emma and Evette were beside him, tears streaming down their faces as they watched helplessly. The paramedics were already at work, their calm efficiency a stark contrast to the chaos of emotion around them.

I knelt by Elijah, becoming a silent pillar of strength for my frightened family. I took Emma's hand, squeezing it tightly, trying to offer some comfort despite my terror.

"It's going to be okay," I whispered, more to myself than to her, my eyes never leaving Elijah as the paramedics stabilized him.

The room was filled with the sounds of medical equipment and soft sobbing. I stayed close, my heart aching as I watched my son, my mind racing with worries about what the future would hold now that this new challenge had surfaced. The joy of the new house was overshadowed by this immediate crisis, reminding me that no matter where we lived, the needs of my family would always come first.

Despite the doctor's dismissive attitude, I refused to let my concerns be silenced. As Elijah underwent further tests and observations, I continued to question the medical staff, advocating for my son's well-being with a determination born from love and maternal instinct.

I pressed the doctors for more thorough examinations, suggesting additional tests to explore potential underlying causes beyond the initial diagnosis of a febrile seizure. With each inquiry, I felt a flicker of defiance ignite within me, a fierce determination to ensure Elijah received the best possible care.

Despite the doctor's skepticism, I remained steadfast, drawing on my knowledge of my son's medical history and the intimate understanding I had cultivated through years of caring for him. I recounted the stressors and transitions our family had faced in recent weeks, highlighting the potential impact on Elijah's health and well-being.

As the medical team reluctantly agreed to run more tests, I felt a glimmer of hope amidst the uncertainty. I knew I had to trust my instincts and continue to advocate fiercely for Elijah, regardless of the skepticism I encountered.

Throughout the ordeal, I leaned on my sister for support, drawing strength from her staunch presence and the reassuring smiles of my other children. Their belief in me and our shared determination to help Elijah through this challenge strengthened my resolve, reminding me that I was not alone in this fight.

Despite the obstacles and doubts that threatened to shake my confidence, I refused to give up on my commitment to my son's well-being. With each test and consultation, I stood firm in my belief that I knew what was best for Elijah, determined to face the challenges ahead with courage and resilience.

After Elijah was released from the hospital, I wasted no time in finding a neurologist to investigate the cause of his seizure. With a determined spirit, I searched the internet and made countless phone calls until I found a highly recommended specialist.

The day of the neurology appointment arrived, and I took Elijah to the doctor's office, my heart heavy with worry but my determination strong. The waiting room was filled with quiet conversations, a backdrop to the nervous anticipation in the air.

When we were called in to see the neurologist, I felt a surge of hope. The doctor greeted us with a warm smile, which immediately put me at ease. He listened carefully as I shared Elijah's medical history, from his early milestones to the recent seizure.

The neurologist nodded thoughtfully, asking detailed questions and taking notes as I spoke. He did a thorough physical exam of Elijah, checking his reflexes, muscle tone, and coordination. With each test, I watched anxiously, my heart skipping a beat with each reassuring nod from the doctor.

After the exam, the neurologist turned to me, his expression serious but kind.

"Based on what you've told me and my examination findings, it's likely that Elijah had a seizure due to a mix of factors, including stress and environmental changes," he explained.

He outlined a comprehensive plan for Elijah's care, which included further tests like an EEG to monitor brain activity and blood work to check for any underlying conditions. He also talked about treatment options, including medication to help manage Elijah's seizures and changes to his lifestyle to reduce triggers.

Throughout the appointment, the neurologist took the time to answer my questions and address my concerns with patience and empathy. He made me feel heard and validated, giving me more confidence in managing Elijah's care.

After our visit, I was hopeful and determined, and just as we were getting ready to leave, the neurologist handed me a piece of paper with contact information for a trusted pediatrician and an autism specialist.

"I've set up appointments for you with these specialists," he said gently.

"I know this is a lot to handle, especially during this time. Consider it one less thing to worry about."

I felt a rush of gratitude towards the neurologist, his thoughtful gesture a lifeline amidst the storm of uncertainty. With a grateful smile, I thanked him, feeling a weight lift from my shoulders knowing that help was on the way.

Over the following days, I received confirmation of the appointments from the neurologist's office. The pediatrician appointment was scheduled for the following week, followed by the autism specialist a few days later.

As I hung up the phone after confirming the appointments, I couldn't help but feel overwhelmed by the support we had received. The kindness and understanding shown by the neurologist reinforced my belief that we were on the right path, with a team of caring professionals guiding us through this challenging time.

With a fresh sense of purpose, I prepared for the upcoming appointments, gathering Elijah's medical records and writing down questions and concerns to discuss with the specialists. Despite the uncertainty that lay ahead, I felt hopeful knowing that we were taking proactive steps towards understanding and managing Elijah's needs.

As the day of the first appointment drew near, I felt a mix of nervousness and anticipation. I knew that the road ahead would be long and challenging, but I also knew that we were not alone. With the support of our new medical team and the unshakable love of my sister, Emma, I was confident that we would navigate this journey, one step at a time.

EIGHT

The day was sunny with clear blue skies. The first appointment with the new pediatrician had me filled with excitement. I was ready to get the twins established with a doctor who took me seriously and genuinely wanted to aid in my kids' care. As the twins and I arrived at the doctor's office, we were greeted by the friendly receptionist and the comfortable waiting room. The colorful walls and soft chairs created a welcoming atmosphere that eased some of my worries.

When we were called in to see Dr. Jameson, I felt both nervous and hopeful. Dr. Jameson welcomed us with a warm smile, making us feel comfortable with his gentle manner. He introduced himself and asked about Evette and Elijah's medical history and any concerns I had.

I told him about Elijah's journey, from his early developmental milestones to his recent seizure. Dr. Jameson listened carefully, nodding as he understood. He asked detailed questions, showing genuine interest in Elijah's well-being. Then, he performed a thorough check-up, examining Elijah's vital signs and growth with care. His kind words and calm demeanor put me at ease.

During the appointment, Dr. Jameson interacted with Elijah, making him feel at ease. He asked Elijah questions and engaged with him in a playful yet professional way, earning a smile and a giggle from my son. This interaction made me feel confident that Dr. Jameson was the right pediatrician for Elijah.

After the examination, Dr. Jameson turned to me with a kind and compassionate look.

"Elijah seems to be doing well overall," he said, which eased my worried heart.

"He's growing and developing slightly below the expected range for his age, but I have no major concerns."

He addressed my worries about the recent seizure, offering reassurance and advice on how to monitor Elijah's health. He reviewed Elijah's chart, noting the neurologist's observations. We talked again about potential triggers and warning signs to watch for, as well as steps to reduce Elijah's risk of another seizure.

Doctor Jameson then turned to Evette who sat quietly keeping Elijah occupied while I was speaking with the doctor. I picked up Elijah from his medical stroller to allow him to stretch while Evette was getting her check-up. Listening intently while continuing to keep Elijah occupied and comfortable as he wanted to stand but still needed quite a bit of support. I was pleased to hear that Evette had a clean bill of health and there were no concerns reported.

As the appointment ended, relief filled my heart. Dr. Jameson's expertise and kindness put me at ease, giving me new confidence in caring for Elijah's health. I thanked the doctor warmly, grateful for his support and guidance. I loaded Elijah back into his stroller, picked up my bags, and took Evette by the hand as we walked out of the treatment room. Passing by the receptionist's desk, the nurse stopped us as we were walking out to ensure the twins both received a sticker of their choice. Leaving the doctor's office, I felt optimistic. As we stepped out into the sunshine, I felt grateful for the bright future that lay ahead with the support of Elijah's medical team and the support of my sister.

A few days later, I took Elijah to see the autism specialist, Dr. Turner. I felt a mix of worry and hope, but Dr. Turner welcomed us warmly. Her office was a calm and quiet place in the busy hospital. She greeted Elijah kindly, making him feel comfortable and valued.

As we started the appointment, Dr. Turner reviewed Elijah's progress since our visit with the pediatrician. She smiled with satisfaction at the progress he had made. Elijah's smile grew as Dr. Turner praised his achievements. Her kind words were a testament to the hard work Elijah and I had put in.

After discussing Elijah's progress, Dr. Turner talked about the next steps for his care. She recommended enrolling Elijah in physical therapy, occupational therapy, and speech therapy once a week. These therapies would help him build strength, improve motor skills, and enhance his communication.

"These therapies will help Elijah grow stronger and improve his skills," Dr. Turner explained, her words filled with hope for Elijah's future. She gave me signed orders for each therapy, making sure I had what I needed to help my son thrive.

Dr. Turner also noticed that Elijah's gait trainer was too small and recommended an evaluation for a new one. She suggested that Elijah be fitted for ankle-foot orthosis (AFO) or supra malleolar orthosis (SMO) braces to support his legs and feet.

"These braces will help Elijah move better and prevent more problems," Dr. Turner assured me. Her expertise and kindness were clear in every word she spoke.

As the appointment ended, I felt grateful. Dr. Turner's recommendations gave us a clear path forward, a plan to help Elijah reach his full potential. With the support of Elijah's medical team and our family, I knew we could face whatever challenges came our way.

Leaving Dr. Turner's office, I was hopeful for Elijah's future. With the therapies and treatments recommended by the specialist, I knew that Elijah would continue to grow and thrive, one step at a time.

As Elijah and I arrived back at Emma's house, we felt a wave of comfort. The familiar sights and sounds of our temporary home offered us peace after all the doctor visits and treatments. Emma greeted us with a warm smile, her presence was always a source of comfort.

But I was determined to get things done. I gathered boxes and packing supplies, keeping my mind on the task. I moved from room to room, sorting through our things and deciding what to take to our new house. Each item I packed reminded me of the journey we had been on and the new adventure we were about to begin.

Elijah watched me with wide eyes, curious about all the activity. I smiled at him, reassuring him with kind words and gentle touches.

"We're getting ready for our new home," I said softly, seeing his excitement grow.

As I packed, memories of our time at Emma's house filled my mind. Each moment reminded me of the love and support we had received. I felt sad about leaving, but I was also excited about starting a new life in our own home.

With each box I filled and labeled, I felt proud. I knew the road ahead would be tough, but I also knew we would face it together, as a family, with love and strength. Emma helped me pack, her support was invaluable during this busy time. As the sun began to set, casting a warm glow over the room, I reflected on our journey. With gratitude in my heart and determination in my soul, I knew the best was yet to come.

When our moving day came, I felt a mix of excitement and nerves. The kids were buzzing with energy as they helped me pack the last of our things into the car. Their laughter and chatter filled the air, adding to the excitement of the day. Despite the chaos of loading boxes and furniture onto the truck, I kept the mood light and fun, telling jokes and playing their favorite music to keep our spirits high. Emma and I worked together seamlessly, our bond strengthening with each task we completed.

As we drove to our new house, I glanced at the kids in the rearview mirror. Their wide-eyed wonder and excitement made me smile. Evette and Elijah chattered about the new home, their imaginations running wild with possibilities.

When we finally arrived at the new house, I pulled into the driveway and watched the kids' faces light up with amazement. The sight of the lawn and the inviting front porch filled them with wonder and adventure. I parked the car, and Evette jumped out to explore. I helped Elijah unbuckle and grabbed his gait trainer from the trunk so he could move around freely. Evette squealed with delight when she saw her new bedroom, while Elijah's eyes sparkled as he touched the smooth walls.

As we settled into our new home, I was deeply grateful. Despite the challenges, we had found a place to call our own—a place where we could create new memories and start new adventures.

As the sun set on our first day, I gathered the kids on the front porch for a snack. Their laughter and chatter filled the air. I looked up at the sky, feeling peace in my heart. At that moment, surrounded by my loved ones, I knew we had found our happy place—a place where we could truly be ourselves and thrive.

Over the weekend, the kids and I were content in our new home. Evette decorated her room with posters and plush toys, while Elijah settled into his space, surrounded by colorful decorations and toys that brought him joy. The house started to feel like home as we added our personal touches to each room.

One of the best parts of the new house was the sunroom I used as a separate playroom for Elijah. It would be a space for him to play and explore, and could also be used as a therapy room, providing him with the support he needed. I spent time organizing the playroom, making sure it was a safe and stimulating environment for Elijah.

With the kids settled, I focused on the practicalities of our new life. I planned to visit the school on Monday to enroll Evette and Elijah and set up services for Elijah's needs. The school was close to our new home and had a special education program that I hoped would accommodate Elijah's needs.

I was relieved to learn that the school had experience with children like Elijah and was committed to supporting him. I scheduled a meeting with the school's special education team to discuss Elijah's Individualized Education Program (IEP) and plan the services and accommodations he would need to succeed. The team seemed understanding and eager to help, which gave me hope.

If Elijah had another seizure, I knew exactly what the school should do. With the help of the neurologist, we made a detailed plan. It included when to give medication when to call for help, and how to keep Elijah safe until medical help arrived. I also made sure the school knew about Elijah's condition and had protocols in place for emergencies. With plans in place, I felt confident and hopeful for our future. Seeing my children's smiling faces, I knew we were where we were meant to be, surrounded by love and possibility.

Walking into the IEP meeting, I felt both nervous and determined. I listened as the school's special education team talked about the services they would offer Elijah. Because Evette and Elijah were in the same class, the school agreed to give Elijah a one-on-one aide. The aide would help him move around, especially during special activities. I felt reassured knowing Elijah would have support.

Three months later, my world was shaken when Evette told me about something that happened in her art class. She saw Elijah alone without his aide, struggling to join the activity. He tried to play with the paint but accidentally knocked it over, making a mess. Instead of helping, the teacher scolded Elijah and made him clean it up himself.

Evette tried to explain that Elijah needed help, but the teacher didn't listen and scolded her for speaking out. Feeling helpless, Evette was sent to the office for what the teacher called *disrespectful behavior*. My heart sank as I listened to Evette's story, filled with anger and worry for her and Elijah.

I immediately took Evette and Elijah to Emma's house, feeling determined. I told Emma about the incident and knew I had to talk to the school about how Elijah was treated, their failure to follow his IEP, and how Evette was treated for trying to protect her brother.

I drove to the school and sat in the car for a few minutes to calm down. I was livid. I took a few deep breaths and I walked into the school. At the front office, I calmly, but firmly said to the secretary,

"I need to speak with the special education director, my son's aide, and the art teacher about what happened with my son yesterday."

The secretary picked up her desk phone and paged each one of the staff members. The director and the aide arrived not long after, their smiles fake.

"Let's go into my office," the director said.

Before I sat down with the director and Elijah's aide, I asked why the art teacher wasn't included in the meeting. The director responded that the art teacher was absent; how convenient. I began to question what took place in the classroom and expected them to downplay the incident. When they did, they kept giving me the runaround, yet not answering any of my questions. I nodded my head and calmly took out a piece of paper from my purse. I handed it to the director and said,

"This is to withdraw my children from the school district. Since my children are not safe here and you and your staff are not following the goals and accommodations implemented in Elijah's IEP, my kids will be homeschooled. Have a great day."

I stood up from my chair, turned toward the door, and walked out of the office, holding my head high but feeling the weight of my decision. I knew it wouldn't be easy, but I was determined to do what was best for my children.

Driving back to Emma's house, I felt relief, but I also had the weight of finances hanging over my head. I knew that money in my account wouldn't last forever. But, I stayed positive and planned to talk to Emma when we arrived at her house. I knew the road ahead would be challenging, but I also knew I made the right choice for my family. With love and determination, I was ready to start this new chapter of our journey together.

Once back at Emma's, I sat down with a cup of tea and took a moment to breathe. I explained that I was somewhat concerned about money running low, especially after deciding to homeschool the kids, which would make it hard for me to work while having them home while helping them with their schoolwork, and Elijah's therapy appointments. I had to make sure that the bills got paid and I had gas to get to all of our doctor's appointments.

Emma always knew what to do in a hard situation. She offered to pay me in the meantime to help her stay organized and do housework for her while she was away on any business meetings for her work. I gratefully took her up on her offer. I knew that Emma would always be there for me no matter what and with the Grace of God I wouldn't have to worry about finances or the lack thereof when it came to my bills.

I knew homeschooling would be a big change, but I felt empowered knowing that I could create a safe and nurturing environment for Evette and Elijah. I started planning our new routine, looking up resources and curriculums that would best suit their needs.

The days that followed were filled with preparation and adjustment. Emma helped me set up a dedicated learning space at her house, where the kids could focus on their studies. I reached out to homeschooling groups and online communities for support and advice. The more I learned, the more confident I felt about this new path we were on.

Elijah and Evette adjusted quickly to the new routine. Our days were structured but flexible, allowing for plenty of one-on-one time and personalized learning. Elijah thrived with individualized attention, making significant progress in his therapies and academics. Evette enjoyed the creative projects and hands-on learning experiences I incorporated into our lessons.

As the weeks turned into months, I saw my children grow and flourish in ways I hadn't anticipated. Homeschooling allowed us to tailor our approach to their unique needs and interests, creating a rich and engaging learning environment. We took field trips, explored nature, and delved into subjects that sparked their curiosity.

Our journey was not without its challenges, but with each obstacle, we found ways to adapt and overcome. The bond between us grew stronger as we navigated this new chapter together. I found solace in the support of other homeschooling parents and the encouragement of friends and family.

One day, as we sat around the table working on a science project, I looked at Elijah and Evette, their faces lit with excitement and wonder. At that moment, I felt overwhelming pride and gratitude. We had faced so many challenges, but we had come through stronger and more determined.

As the seasons changed and we settled into our new routine, I knew that this was just the beginning of a beautiful journey. With love, determination, and the support of my sister, I was ready to face whatever came my way. Together, my family would continue to grow, learn, and thrive, one step at a time.

NINE

Months had passed since I decided to homeschool Evette and Elijah. At first, I felt overwhelmed by taking on my children's education, but soon I found my way and established a steady routine. The journey from feeling unsure to feeling capable wasn't easy. Each day brought its challenges, from planning lessons to keeping the kids engaged and motivated. Yet, as I faced these hurdles, I discovered a deep fulfillment that I didn't expect.

Every morning, as they gathered around the kitchen table turned classroom, I felt joy in seeing the spark of understanding in my children's eyes. We covered different subjects, from math, where they worked on numbers and patterns, to literature, where we explored magical worlds in stories. Each lesson was a chance not just to teach but to grow closer to my children.

I carefully chose a curriculum that met educational standards and also matched Evette's curiosity and Elijah's unique learning needs. This personalized approach let each child grow at their own pace, something traditional schools had struggled to do. Watching Evette solve a tough problem on her own or hearing Elijah read aloud with more confidence reinforced my belief in the path I had chosen.

Homeschooling also brought unexpected joys. Projects and experiments became family activities, and trips to local museums or parks became part of our learning. These experiences enriched the children's education and added a hands-on aspect that books alone couldn't provide.

As we went through these moments, my initial worries faded, replaced by confidence in my teaching and a deep appreciation for understanding my children's thoughts and dreams. The challenges of homeschooling were still there, but they were small compared to the rewards of seeing Evette and Elijah thrive under my guidance. This journey had not only changed their learning but had also deepened our family bonds, bringing us closer with each lesson and discovery.

While balancing household chores and lesson plans, I marveled at Evette and Elijah's progress. Evette worked hard on her sight words, her determination clear as she practiced with enthusiasm. Meanwhile, Elijah eagerly explored letters and sounds, his curiosity driving him to learn new words and ideas.

As lunchtime approached, I called the kids to the kitchen. Their morning of learning had made them hungry. With gentle reminders to wash their hands and sit at the table, I served lunch and smiled as they ate with gusto.

After lunch, I took the kids to their bedrooms for a nap. With soft kisses and soothing words, I tucked them in, watching with satisfaction as they drifted off to sleep, their dreams filled with the day's wonders.

As the house grew quiet, I paused to reflect on our journey together. Despite the challenges ahead, I knew we were where we were meant to be—learning and growing together, one day at a time.

With fresh energy, I tackled my tasks, my mind filled with plans and dreams for the future. In the quiet moments of the afternoon, amidst the daily hustle, I found peace and purpose that filled my heart with joy.

As the afternoon wore on, I couldn't stop thinking about the mysterious letter that arrived in the mailbox earlier that morning. Despite my efforts to focus, my mind kept wandering back to the letter's unanswered questions.

While doing my chores, my thoughts returned to the unopened letter on the kitchen counter. It looked ordinary, but its unannounced arrival and unknown sender made it mysterious. Who could it be from? And what news did it hold? These questions nagged at me more and more.

Was the letter simply misdelivered, containing boring details meant for someone else? Or was it something more interesting or even scary? The thought of a hidden message made me feel like I was about to discover something important. This gave me a mix of excitement and nervousness.

With each passing hour, as I folded laundry and washed dishes, my curiosity grew. It tugged at me, pulling my attention back to the mystery of the unopened envelope. I imagined scenarios ranging from long-lost relatives reaching out to old friends sharing unexpected news or secrets.

After a day full of distractions and growing curiosity, I could no longer resist the urge to discover the letter's contents. The intrigue that had built up all day was too intense, and my resolve finally crumbled. I found myself drawn back to the kitchen, where the letter lay on the counter, an object that seemed to have immense power over my emotions.

This growing obsession made it harder for me to focus on my daily tasks. I found myself stopping mid-task, lost in thought, my hands idle as my mind raced with possibilities. The letter seemed to call to me, urging me to open it and see what it said. Yet, part of me hesitated, driven by a mix of fear and excitement about what it might reveal.

In the end, the feeling of the unknown was too strong to ignore. I realized that the only way to ease my mind was to confront the letter I received head-on, to open it and see what message it carried. Once I made this decision, I felt a bit relieved, mixed with eager anticipation as I prepared to uncover the secrets hidden in the mysterious letter.

As I walked to the counter, my steps were slow but determined. The letter, once just a piece of paper, now felt like a gateway to something unknown, maybe important. With each step closer, my heart beat faster, a mix of nervousness and excitement taking hold. This moment felt bigger than just reading a letter; it felt like stepping into a new and unknown chapter.

Standing in front of the counter, I paused for a moment, gathering my courage. My hands, slightly shaking from the mix of emotions inside me, reached for the envelope. The paper felt surprisingly firm under my fingers, adding a feeling of gravity to the moment. Carefully, as if handling a delicate treasure, I began to tear open the envelope, my movements slow and deliberate to avoid ripping the contents inside.

As the seal broke and the flap lifted, my heart raced even faster, pounding against my chest with anticipation. What secrets lay hidden within these folds? What message had traveled through the mail to land on my kitchen counter? With a deep breath, I widened the opening, pulling out the contents to finally reveal the mystery that had consumed my day. The moment of truth was upon me, and every nerve in my body was alert, ready to absorb the impact of the words I was about to read.

As I carefully unfolded the letter, my eyes widened in surprise at what I saw inside. Spread out before me were several scriptures, neatly printed on parchment-like paper. The words were full of peace and wisdom and touched me deeply.

Each verse spoke to me differently, offering comfort, guidance, and hope during life's challenges.

As I read them, I felt a strong purpose fill me, as if each word was meant just for me.

Alongside the scriptures, inside the letter, was a trifold brochure with pictures of a quaint church among the trees. The brochure detailed the various services and programs offered by the church, from Sunday worship services to Bible study groups and community outreach.

As I read through the brochure, I felt drawn to the warmth and welcome from its pages. It was as if the church was inviting me to come and explore the faith and fellowship waiting for me within its walls.

With a feeling of curiosity and excitement, I tucked the letter and brochure into my purse, knowing that I had found something special—a message of hope and encouragement that had come to me in the most unexpected way.

As I thought about the letter and its contents, I couldn't shake the feeling that this was just the beginning of a new chapter in my life—a chapter filled with faith, community, and the promise of a brighter tomorrow.

That night, I took the letter out of my purse. I looked deeper into the scriptures inside the letter, and I found myself drawn to the wisdom and truths they held. Each verse uniquely spoke to me, offering comfort and guidance amid life's uncertainties.

One verse, in particular, touched me deeply:

"Trust in the Lord with all your heart and lean not on your own understanding; in all your ways submit to him, and he will make your paths straight. - Proverbs 3:5-6"

As I thought about those words, I felt a wave of peace wash over me, as if the burdens I had been carrying were suddenly lifted from my shoulders. In a world filled with chaos and confusion, this verse reminded me to trust in God's plan and to let Him take control, knowing that He would always guide me in the right direction.

Another verse that spoke to my heart was:

"For I know the plans I have for you, declares the Lord, plans to prosper you and not to harm you, plans to give you hope and a future. - Jeremiah 29:11"

As I read those words, I felt hope and purpose growing inside me. Despite the challenges I had faced, I knew that God had a plan for my life—a plan filled with blessings and opportunities that far exceeded anything I could ever imagine.

With each scripture I encountered, I felt my faith growing and my spirit lifting, as if I were being guided by an unseen hand toward a brighter tomorrow. These words were more than just ink on paper; they were a lifeline, a source of strength and encouragement that sustained me through the darkest of days.

As I thought about the meaning behind the scriptures within the letter, I realized that this was more than just a coincidence—it was a divine message, a reminder that I was never alone and that God was always by my side, guiding my every step.

As I thought about the scriptures and the invitation from the church, I couldn't help but acknowledge my journey with faith. Growing up, I had never been one to attend church regularly. My parents were not the church-going type, and the topic of religion was rarely discussed in our house.

Despite that, I had always felt a deep sense of curiosity and longing to know more about God and spirituality. I believed in God and had a strong desire to deepen my faith, but the chance to explore these beliefs further had never come—until now.

The letter and the scriptures it contained felt like a divine intervention, a gentle nudge from above urging me to embark on a new path of spiritual discovery. It was as if God Himself was reaching out to me, inviting me to come and experience His love and grace in a way I had never known before.

As I thought about the invitation from the church, I felt a stirring within my soul—a yearning to explore the depths of faith and to connect with others who shared my beliefs. It was a chance to step out of my comfort zone, embrace the unknown, and open myself up to the possibility of experiencing God in a whole new way.

With excitement and anticipation running through me, I decided to accept the invitation from the church. It was a leap of faith, a step into the unknown, but I knew it was worth it. This journey would bring my children and me closer to God and help us understand His love and purpose for our lives.

With a mix of excitement and nervousness, I picked up the phone and dialed Emma's number, eager to share the news about the letter and the invitation from the church. As the phone rang, my heart pounded in my chest, anticipation building with each passing moment.

"Hello?"

Emma's familiar voice greeted me on the other end of the line, warm and welcoming as always.

"Hey, Emma, it's me," I began, my voice tinged with excitement.

"I have something I need to tell you."

As I recounted the events of the day—the mysterious letter, the scriptures it contained, and the invitation from the church—I could practically hear the smile spreading across Emma's face on the other end of the line.

"Wow, Evelyn, that's incredible!" Emma exclaimed, her voice filled with genuine excitement.

"I'm so happy for you! This sounds like the start of something amazing."

I couldn't help but feel a surge of gratitude wash over me as I listened to Emma's words of encouragement.

"Thank you, Emma," I replied, my voice beginning to choke with emotion.

"I'm just so grateful for this opportunity to explore my faith and to connect with others who share my beliefs. It feels like a gift, you know?"

"I know exactly what you mean, Evelyn," Emma said softly.

"And I'm here for you every step of the way. We'll figure this out together."

With a new purpose and determination, I hung up the phone, my heart lighter than it had been in months. I knew this journey would not be easy, but with Emma by my side and God guiding me, I was ready to face whatever lay ahead.

TEN

With a mix of nerves and excitement, I decided to go to the Sunday service at the church with Emma and the kids. It was a step into the unknown, but I knew it was a journey worth taking. It promised a new faith and a strong feeling of belonging.

On a bright Sunday morning, sunlight streamed through the windows of my home, casting a warm glow over the living room where the kids and I were getting ready for church. Excitement was in the air as I helped Evette and Elijah into their Sunday best, smoothing their hair and straightening their collars with gentle hands.

As I slipped into my dress, I felt a flutter of nerves in my stomach. Attending church with Emma and the kids was new to me, and I wanted everything to go smoothly. Taking a deep breath, I reminded myself of the purpose and determination that had brought me to this moment. It was a moment of faith and community that I knew would shape our journey in profound ways.

With everyone dressed and ready, I gathered the kids' belongings and ushered them out the door. The excitement of the day was palpable. As they climbed into the car, I felt some anticipation and wondered what the day would bring.

The drive to the church was short, with the vibrant colors of spring painting the landscape. It wasn't long before we arrived at the church, its sight glowed before us like roars of hope and belonging.

As we pulled into the parking lot, I was struck by the size and grandeur of the church. Its tall spire reached toward the sky, a testament to the faith and devotion of its congregation. With its welcoming wooden doors, and shiny brass handles, I began to feel the excitement bubbling up inside me—a feeling of belonging I hadn't felt in a long time.

With a smile and a heart full of hope, I led the kids towards the entrance of the church, ready to start this new chapter of our journey. As we stepped through the doors and into the welcoming embrace of the church community, I knew we were exactly where we were meant to be—a family united in faith and love, ready to explore God's grace together.

As we entered the church, I could feel the peace come over me. The sound of hymns filled the air, and the congregation's warm smiles welcomed us inside. Emma squeezed my hand reassuringly, her presence a source of comfort and strength as we made our way to our seats.

The kids, wide-eyed with curiosity, took in their surroundings with wonder and awe. Evette whispered excitedly to Elijah, pointing out the colorful stained glass windows and the intricate details of the altar. Elijah gazed around with curiosity and fascination in his eyes.

Just before the service began, I was pleasantly surprised by how welcoming the church was to families with young children. The kids were invited to join in various activities during the service, from singing worship songs to age-appropriate lessons and crafts.

Evette eagerly joined the other children in the children's ministry, her face lit up with joy as she made new friends and explored stories of faith through interactive lessons and games. Meanwhile, Elijah, with the help of a kind volunteer from the church, participated in a sensory-friendly activity tailored to his needs, his smile lighting up the room as he engaged with the materials before him.

As I watched my children immerse themselves in the church community, I was grateful. I deeply appreciated the inclusive and nurturing environment that welcomed us with open arms. It was a moment I would never forget, reaffirming my decision to take this journey of faith and discovery with my family.

As Emma and I made our way through the bustling sanctuary, we were greeted with warm smiles and friendly greetings from the congregation. It was clear from the moment we stepped inside that we were welcomed with open arms, and embraced as part of the church family.

As we found our seats among the rows of pews, I noticed how everyone seemed like good friends, and it made me happy. Everywhere I looked, people were engaged in conversation, sharing stories and laughter.

Emma, ever the social butterfly, quickly struck up conversations with those around us, introducing herself and me and eagerly sharing our story of how we came to find the church. The response from the congregation was overwhelmingly positive, with many expressing their excitement at welcoming new members into the fold.

During the service, Emma and I felt like we were part of a big family, which made us feel genuinely accepted. From the heartfelt worship songs to the pastor's words of encouragement and support, we felt uplifted and inspired by the love and fellowship around us.

When the service ended, we stayed behind in the sanctuary, chatting with members of the congregation. Emma and I couldn't help but feel grateful for the connections we had made. It was clear we had found more than just a place to worship—we had found a family, a community of faith and love that would support us through life's ups and downs.

As we said our goodbyes and walked to the car, I couldn't stop smiling, my heart was bursting with love and joy. It was a feeling I knew we would carry with us long after we left the church that day—a feeling of belonging, of being truly seen and accepted for who we were.

As the service ended, I felt really peaceful and happy inside. I knew this was just the start of our time with the church—a time filled with love, friendship, and hope for the future.

As we drove home, Emma and I reflected on the loving community we had found at the church and the deep connections we had made with its members. We knew we had found a home—a place where we could grow in our faith and share our journey with others who walked beside us.

As Sunday morning came once again, the kids and I eagerly prepared to attend church, our hearts full of anticipation for the fellowship and worship that awaited us. With each passing week, we grew more deeply connected to the church community, finding solace and strength in the shared experience of faith and love.

As we walked into the sanctuary, I felt calm—a calmness that seemed to spread all around us. The sanctuary was filled with music and laughter, everyone's happy voices were harmonizing as they sang and prayed.

As the service began, I got the kids settled in the Sunday school room and then took my seat back in the sanctuary. My eyes fixed on the pulpit where the pastor stood, ready to deliver his message. The day's sermon was about forgiveness—a topic that struck a chord with me as I listened to the pastor's words.

With a mix of vulnerability and grace, the pastor shared stories about the power of forgiveness in our lives, urging us to let go of bitterness and embrace the healing power of love. His words resonated deeply with me, stirring something in my soul as I thought about my journey toward forgiveness and healing with Michael.

Throughout the service, the kids and I were engaged and attentive, our hearts open to the message of hope and redemption.

When the service finished and we headed home, I just felt thankful—thankful for getting to pray with my kids and be part of a group that made us feel so welcome.

On the way home, the kids and I talked about the message we had heard. We discussed the importance of forgiveness in our own lives, sharing stories and insights. It was a moment of connection and growth—a reminder of the power of faith and love to change our lives and the world around us.

After getting home from church, I felt a strong urge inside me—a deep longing to take the next step in my spiritual journey. With a strong feeling in my heart, I called Emma, excited to tell her about my new determination and drive.

As the phone rang, my heart raced, my thoughts running ahead to what I would say. When Emma's voice greeted me, warm and welcoming as always, I felt a surge of relief wash over me.

"Hey, Emma, it's me," I began, my voice tinged with excitement.

"I have something I need to tell you."

As I told Emma about my desire to get baptized, I felt a little vulnerable. The type of vulnerability that I knew I could trust Emma to handle with care. Emma listened closely, offering words of support and encouragement that soothed my soul.

"That's incredible, Evelyn," Emma exclaimed, her voice filled with genuine excitement.

"I'm so proud of you! This is such a meaningful step in your faith journey, and I know it will be a beautiful and transformative experience for you."

I couldn't help but feel thankful for my sister. Her constant support gave me strength and comfort. With Emma by my side, I felt brave enough to start this new part of my spiritual journey.

As we kept talking, Emma and I shared stories about our faith. Our bond grew stronger with every word. It was a talk filled with love and understanding. It reminded me how much I needed my sister and how important it was to have someone with me on this journey. Emma said she was happy about my newfound determination and belief in my faith. Even in our serious conversation, Emma managed to make me laugh with her playful personality.

"That's wonderful, Evelyn," Emma said, her voice full of excitement.

"Who knows, maybe you'll even find a nice new husband at the church!"

I couldn't help but laugh at Emma's joke, my cheeks turning red with amusement. It was a light moment in our serious talk, reminding me of Emma's fun spirit and her talent for finding humor in everything.

"Emma, you always know how to make me smile," I said, laughing.

"But for now, I think I'll focus on my relationship with God before I start thinking about finding a new husband!"

We shared a smile, our bond stronger with the shared laughter. Moments like these reminded me why having Emma by my side was so important—a sister who could lift my spirits and bring joy even during serious times. As we kept talking, I felt a deep gratitude for the connection I shared with my sister and the moments of joy and laughter we had. With Emma's love and support, I knew I could face any challenge.

When we said our goodbyes and ended the call, I felt excitement growing inside me. I was looking forward to the journey ahead and the adventures waiting for me in the church. With Emma's playful joke in my mind, I knew I was ready to welcome whatever the future held with open arms and a happy heart.

With a new purpose and determination, I focused on the path before me. I was ready to take the next step in my faith journey with courage. And with Emma's love and support, I knew I could embrace whatever lay ahead with open arms.

ELEVEN

As the sun began to peek through the curtains, casting a soft glow over the room, I woke up, the excitement of the day already stirring within me. With a yawn and a stretch, I swung my legs out of bed, ready to start the day.

After a quick breakfast of pancakes and fresh fruit, I gathered the kids, their laughter filling the air as they chatted excitedly about the day ahead. Evette and Elijah were eager to go to church and see Pastor George again. Their faces lit up with excitement as they talked about the stories and songs they would hear.

With breakfast finished and teeth brushed, I helped the kids into their Sunday best, smoothing down their hair and straightening their collars. Evette twirled in front of the mirror, her dress swirling around her legs as she giggled. Elijah beamed proudly in his little suit, his eyes shining with excitement.

As we got into the car and fastened our seat belts, I felt happy and satisfied. We were embarking on a journey of faith together as a family. With the engine purring beneath us, we set off towards the church, the road stretching out before us like a ribbon of promise.

The drive to church was short, the familiar sights and sounds of our neighborhood passing by in a blur. As we pulled into the parking lot of the church, I felt a flutter of excitement in my stomach, anticipating the adventures that awaited us inside.

Stepping out of the car, I took a moment to gather myself, my heart pounding with nervous excitement at the thought of meeting Pastor George for the first time. With a deep breath and a smile on my face, I reached out to take Evette and Elijah's hands. Their warmth and presence gave me strength and comfort as we walked toward the entrance of the church.

As we entered the sanctuary, the sounds of music and laughter washed over us, filling the air with joy and celebration. I felt calm and happy as I glanced at the friendly faces of the church members, their smiles making us feel at home. We found our seats and got ready to pray as a family. I was thankful to be here with my kids, starting this faith journey together.

The church service had just ended, the last notes of the closing hymn still lingering in the air as the congregation began to disperse. The lively chatter of the community filled the room, making me feel right at home. Holding Elijah's hand tightly, I led Evette and him toward Pastor George, who was surrounded by a few people.

Pastor George's eyes brightened as he saw us coming. His smile was wide, his arms open as if ready to embrace the whole world.

"Ah, here are some new faces!" he exclaimed. I introduced myself and the twins, my voice was soft but strong from the morning's sermon.

"I'm Evelyn, and these are my twins, Evette and Elijah. We really enjoyed your sermon today."

"It's a blessing to meet you all," Pastor George said, bending down to be at eye level with Evette and Elijah.

"And what beautiful names! Evette, like a little poet, and Elijah, strong and brave."

Evette shyly hid behind me, peeking out just enough to study Pastor George. Elijah, however, looked up at the pastor, a small smile on his lips, encouraged by the kindness in the pastor's eyes.

Pastor George straightened up, turning back to me.

"And what brings you to our little family here at Abundant Life Church?" he asked.

I felt warmth spread through my chest, my decision feeling right.

"I've been looking for a place where we can grow and find community," I admitted.

"And... I've been thinking about baptism. I feel it's time to renew my faith and start a new chapter for us as a family."

Pastor George's smile deepened, his eyes twinkling.

"That's wonderful, Evelyn. There's nothing more beautiful than a heart open to God's grace and new beginnings. We will support you every step of the way."

He then looked down at Elijah, who had been quietly listening. Kneeling, Pastor George placed a gentle hand on Elijah's shoulder.

"Young man, may I pray for you?" he asked softly.

I nodded, squeezing Elijah's hand for encouragement. Elijah glanced at me, then back at Pastor George, giving a small nod.

Pastor George closed his eyes, his other hand reaching out to include Evette and me in his prayer.

"Heavenly Father," he began,

"We thank You for bringing Evelyn and her wonderful children into our family today. We ask for Your healing touch on young Elijah, that he may feel Your strength and love every day. Bless this family, Lord, with Your peace and joy. In Jesus' name, we pray. Amen."

As we opened our eyes, there was a quiet moment that seemed to wrap around us like a gentle hug. My eyes were moist with tears of gratitude, touched by the genuine care and prayer offered for my son.

"Thank you, Pastor George," I whispered, my heart full.

"Welcome to Abundant Life Church," Pastor George replied, standing up with a reassuring pat on Elijah's back.

"We're so glad you're here."

As we walked back to our seats, I felt a lightness in my step, a peace in my heart that I hadn't felt in a long time. It was the beginning of something beautiful, a new chapter not just in my spiritual life but for my family as well. I knew we had found a place to belong, a community to grow with, and a pastor who truly cared.

As the congregation began to leave the chapel, Pastor George caught up with me and the twins, a thoughtful look on his face.

"Evelyn, before you leave, may I have a moment?" he asked gently.

I turned, my face open and curious.

"Of course, Pastor George," I responded.

"I was thinking about your visit next week for your baptism," he began, his eyes reflecting sincere care.

"It's a wonderful step you're taking, and I believe it could be made even more special with a little extra support for your family."

I nodded, my interest growing.

"What do you have in mind?"

Pastor George smiled, his excitement clear.

"We have a great Children's Youth Pastor here, Christopher. He runs a special program for the kids. I think it could really help Elijah, and Evette is welcome to join too."

My eyes lit up at the thought of something that could help Elijah. I always looked for ways to support him, knowing each step forward was important.

"That sounds wonderful. What kind of program is it?"

"I'll let Christopher tell you all the details next week," Pastor George said, his smile reassuring.

"He's better at explaining how it works. He connects well with the children and makes a real impact. Plus, his own son, Lorenzo, is part of the program, which adds a nice personal touch."

The idea of a program for children like Elijah, run by someone who understood their needs, filled me with hope.

"I'll definitely be here," I said, my voice steady and determined.

"It sounds like just what Elijah needs, and I'm sure Evette will enjoy it too."

"Excellent!" Pastor George clapped his hands, pleased.

"After your baptism, I'll introduce you to Christopher, and you can discuss everything in detail."

Just as we were about to part ways, I asked Pastor George about the life coaching services that were displayed in the trifold I had received. I had been to counseling for a few months, and that did seem to help, but I wanted something more. I wanted something that would help me navigate the future for not only me but for the twins as well. Pastor George immediately waved his wife to come over to where we were standing and introduced me to her.

"Evelyn, this is my wife, Carry. She would be the perfect person to talk to as she is the life coach here at Abundant Life Church, and she can answer any questions you may have, and how to get started with her."

I felt a surge of excitement for the coming week. Not only was I taking a big step in my faith journey by getting baptized, and preparing for classes with my new life coach, but I was also opening a door to new opportunities for my children.

As the doors of Abundant Life Church closed behind us, I stepped into the bright sunlight, my twins at my side. The morning had unfolded in a way that left my heart light and hopeful. With Elijah's hand firmly in mine and Evette skipping ahead, I led them to our car parked under a nearby oak tree.

I secured Elijah in his seat, making sure his seatbelt was comfortable, and did the same for Evette, who was still buzzing with excitement. Once everyone was settled, I slid into the driver's seat, taking a moment to collect my thoughts.

As I started the engine, the car filled with the light chatter of my children, discussing their favorite parts of the morning. Evette loved the music, humming bits of the last hymn, while Elijah seemed quieter but content, his eyes meeting mine in the rearview mirror with a gentle happiness.

The drive home was smooth, with the streets less crowded than usual. My mind wandered to the upcoming baptism and the talk I would have with Pastor Christopher about his program. I felt a mix of excitement and nervousness about introducing Elijah and Evette to a new environment, hoping it would be a place where they could thrive and feel accepted. But, my heart was full of hope, eager for what lay ahead, knowing I was paving a path toward growth and healing for my family.

As we turned onto our street, the familiar sights of neatly trimmed lawns and colorful flower beds greeted us. Home always brought us peace and stability, and today it seemed to promise new beginnings as well.

Pulling into the driveway, I helped the twins out of the car, and they headed to the front door together.

"Mom, can we have pancakes for lunch?" Evette asked, her eyes sparkling with the hopeful excitement of a child who believes pancakes are good at any hour. I laughed.

"Pancakes sound perfect," I replied, ruffling Evette's hair.

Elijah clapped his hands, clearly happy with the choice.

As we entered the house, the familiar comfort of home wrapped around us. I felt grateful for the support we'd found at church, the upcoming opportunities for my children, and the small family moments like making pancakes on a Sunday afternoon. Today, more than ever, I felt anchored in my faith and my role as a mother, ready to face whatever challenges and joys lay ahead.

In the warm kitchen, the scent of freshly made pancakes filled the air. I stood by the stove, flipping pancakes until they were golden, my movements sure. Evette and Elijah sat eagerly at the table, their faces lit up with the simple joy that only a surprise pancake lunch could bring.

Once the pancakes were ready, I placed them on plates, drizzled them with syrup, and added a few slices of banana on the side.

"Eat up," I smiled, watching my children dive into their meal with delight.

The laughter and chatter filled the kitchen as we ate. I joined in, sharing stories and listening to the twins talk about their morning. It was moments like these, in the simple day-to-day, where I found my greatest joy.

After we cleared the plates and tidied up the kitchen, I took the children to the living room. They settled with their coloring books and toys, giving me a moment to sit at the dining table with a fresh cup of coffee and a notepad. It was time to organize my thoughts and tasks for the upcoming week.

I wrote at the top of the pad, 'Week's Goals,' and began listing:

- Baptism Preparation: Choose a dress for the baptism, and confirm the time with Pastor George.

- Meet with Pastor Christopher: Learn more about the children's program, especially any specific ways it might help Elijah.

- Grocery Shopping: Stock up on healthy snacks and meal prep ingredients.

- Homeschool Prep: Organize learning activities for the week, focusing on math for Evette and sensory activities for Elijah.

- Exercise: Find thirty minutes each day for a walk or home workout.

- Family Time: Plan a fun activity for the weekend. Maybe a visit to the local park or a movie night.

As I wrote, each task felt like a small commitment to my family's future and my growth. I knew that balancing my goals as a mother and an author was hard, but it was a challenge I embraced fully. Once the list was complete, I felt a surge of productivity and optimism. With everything laid out so clearly, I felt ready to tackle the week ahead, confident in my ability to manage my time and prioritize my family's needs.

With a final sip of my coffee, I folded the notepad, my mind already ticking through the tasks as I moved to join my children in the living room, my heart content and my purpose clear.

TWELVE

Early Monday morning, as the first rays of sunlight gently filtered through the curtains, casting a soft glow across the room, I stood before my open closet. The task ahead was simple yet important—choosing the perfect outfit for my baptism this coming Sunday. I ran my fingers over the fabrics, each piece telling a story of past occasions, moments of joy, and celebrations. Today, I needed something special, a dress that would be modest for church but also a bit festive.

I paused, thinking about the different dresses. There was the deep green one I wore at a friend's wedding, too formal and serious for the occasion. Then, my hand brushed against a soft blue fabric, light and airy, hanging almost hidden behind my everyday clothes. Pulling it out, I held it up against the morning light, seeing how the fabric seemed to dance in the gentle breeze from the window. The dress was simple, with a modest neckline and short sleeves, the skirt flowing loosely just below my knees—perfect for the solemnity and joy of a baptism.

Turning to the full-length mirror, I slipped the dress over my head, the fabric settling comfortably over my frame. It was just the right balance of elegance and comfort. The soft blue reminded me of a clear sky on a sunny day, hopeful and serene, reflecting my feelings about reaffirming my faith. I chose a delicate silver necklace with a small cross pendant, a symbol of my dedication and belief.

Satisfied with my choice, I hung the dress on the outside of my closet door, positioning it so it was the first thing I would see when I woke up Sunday morning. Below it, I placed a pair of white flats, simple and practical for the occasion. The outfit, carefully selected and prepared, served as a visual reminder of the important step I was about to take in my faith journey. It was not just about the looks; it was a declaration of my commitment to my path, a celebration of a new chapter in my spiritual life.

As I stepped back to look at the outfit, my heart was filled with a mix of anticipation and peace. A baptism symbolizes a fresh start, a washing away of the old, and a rebirth in my devotion and life's purpose. With a deep, contented breath, I turned away from the wardrobe, ready to start my day, my thoughts already on the ceremony and the personal change it represented.

Wednesday dawned bright and clear, the perfect day for my weekly grocery run. I woke up early, energized by the thought of filling my pantry and fridge with nutritious foods that would nourish my family throughout the coming week. After a light breakfast with the twins, I loaded them into the car, their chatter filling the space with excitement about helping Mommy pick out the best fruits and snacks.

Arriving at the supermarket, I grabbed a shopping cart and together with Evette and Elijah, entered the bustling store. The bright fluorescent lights illuminated rows of fresh produce, canned goods, and everything in between. I pulled out the shopping list I had made the night before, my pen ready to check off items as we loaded them into the cart.

The first stop was the produce section. I guided the twins through the colorful fruits and vegetables, explaining the health benefits of each.

"These oranges are like little suns packed with vitamin C," I told them, picking up a few to check their firmness.

They filled bags with leafy greens, bell peppers in a rainbow of colors, and sweet, plump tomatoes. Evette was particularly excited to choose the apples, picking a variety of red, green, and yellow, each one checked for its crispness.

Next, we went to the meats, where I selected lean cuts of chicken and turkey, along with some salmon that shone under the store's lights.

"Fish is good for your brain," I explained to Elijah, who looked curiously at the silvery scales.

I also picked up some plant-based proteins, including lentils and chickpeas, planning to make a hearty stew later in the week.

As we continued through the aisles, I added whole grains like quinoa and brown rice to the cart, along with dairy products—yogurt and cheese, carefully choosing the low-fat options. I talked with the twins about the importance of balance in their diet, making the shopping trip both educational and fun.

We spent a good part of the morning exploring the aisles, with me teaching the twins how to read nutrition labels and choose snacks that were healthy but still tasty. By the time we reached the checkout, the cart was brimming with wholesome food, and the twins were proud of their choices.

After paying, we headed to the car, and I organized the bags in the trunk with systematic precision. Each bag was packed so that nothing would be crushed on the drive home. As I closed the trunk, a deep sense of satisfaction settled over me. I had not only stocked up on healthy food but had also turned the grocery trip into a learning experience for Evette and Elijah.

Driving back home, I felt a quiet pride in my heart. I was making thoughtful, informed choices to ensure my family's health and happiness. This grocery trip was more than just a weekly chore; it was a cornerstone of their healthy lifestyle, and I was pleased to see my efforts coming to life, one meal at a time.

Thursday morning arrived with a soft, gentle light filtering through the windows of my dining room, setting a calm and focused atmosphere for the day's task. As the children enjoyed a leisurely breakfast, I prepared for an important part of my week: planning the homeschool activities. This was a task I took seriously and approached with creativity, knowing how important these years were for Evette and Elijah.

With the breakfast dishes cleared away and the twins settled into their playroom, I turned my attention to the large dining table that now served as my planning station. I spread out all the educational materials I had gathered over the week—a mix of bought resources and some I had made myself. For Evette, there were several math workbooks covering topics from basic arithmetic to more challenging problem-solving exercises to build her numerical skills and logical thinking. Alongside these, I laid out reading comprehension books and science kits that would let Evette explore the natural world and develop her literacy skills.

For Elijah, I prepared a variety of sensory bins filled with materials like sand, water beads, and rice. Each bin had a theme to not only stimulate his sensory processing but also to teach him about different environments like the ocean, the forest, and the desert. I included small toys and objects related to each theme, which would help Elijah connect the sensory experience with real-world concepts.

I also set out visual aids, flashcards, and interactive games that would cater to Elijah's learning needs, focusing on improving his communication skills and expanding his ability to follow instructions through fun and hands-on activities.

Once all the materials were laid out, I began the process of organizing each day's activities into labeled folders. I created a detailed schedule, setting time for each subject and making sure both children would have a balanced day with periods of learning, play, and rest. For Evette, I mixed math lessons with science experiments and story-reading sessions, while for Elijah, I mixed sensory play with simple puzzles and picture-based storytime.

As I labeled each folder, I felt excited about the week ahead. I imagined how Evette might light up as she discovered a new scientific concept or solved a hard math problem. I pictured Elijah's joy and focus as he explored a new sensory bin, his hands busy and his mind engaged.

This planning session was more than just a routine—it was a labor of love, an investment in my children's future. I knew that these home-based educational activities were important, not just for academic growth but for nurturing a love of learning in my children. Each labeled folder represented a day of opportunities, challenges, and discoveries that I and my children would explore together.

With the folders neatly stacked and the table cleared, I stepped back, a satisfied smile crossing my face. I was ready for another week of homeschooling, armed with well-planned activities and fueled by the joy of teaching my children in such a personal, hands-on manner. This was not just education; it was a journey we were on together, each day bringing us closer, one learning moment at a time.

Despite my busy week, which was filled with homeschooling, house chores, Elijah's therapy, and my projects, I always made sure to carve out time for my health and well-being. This Friday was no exception. After finishing the morning chores and seeing the twins happily engaged with their puzzles and books, and waiting for their Aunt Emma to arrive, I took a moment for myself—a necessary pause in my busy routine.

I went to my bedroom and pulled out my favorite pair of sneakers, the well-worn soles showing signs of many previous mornings like this. As I tied the laces, my mind began to ease from the many tasks awaiting my return. This was my time, a precious half-hour where my only job was to breathe and move.

As I stepped out of the house, I was greeted by Emma who had just closed her car door, walking inside. In passing, I hugged her, thanked her for watching the twins for me, and then began to walk down the driveway. There was a cool breeze, a gentle reminder of the autumn season slowly taking hold of my neighborhood. The leaves had begun to change, painting the suburban landscape in shades of amber and gold, a natural mosaic that promised a beautiful backdrop for my walk.

I started down my usual path, a well-trodden route through the quieter streets of my neighborhood, where familiar houses stood like old friends. With each step, I felt my muscles warming, my breath deepening, and my thoughts slowly drifting away from the daily grind. The rhythm of my footsteps became a calming beat, grounding me in the present moment.

As I walked, I took in the sights and sounds around me—the chirping of birds preparing for migration, the rustle of leaves underfoot, and the distant laughter of children playing in a nearby park. I passed Mrs. Jones, who was tending to her rose bushes, exchanging a friendly wave and a few words about the changing weather. These small interactions, brief as they were, connected me to the community and reminded me that I was part of a larger world.

Halfway through my walk, I reached the top of a small hill, the highest point in my route, which gave me a wide view of my neighborhood. I paused, taking a moment to catch my breath and enjoy the view. From here, the world seemed peaceful and orderly, a big difference from the chaos that sometimes filled my days. It was a visual reward for my efforts, both on this walk and in my life.

Feeling refreshed by the scene, I started walking again, now at a faster pace. The return journey always seemed quicker, my body fully awake and my mind clear. This walk was not just a break from my duties but a reminder of my commitment to myself. It was a way to show that despite the demands of being a mother and teacher, I too deserved care and attention.

By the time I walked back through my front door, I was refreshed and rejuvenated. The simple act of taking a brisk walk got rid of any lingering stress and reminded me of the importance of my health and well-being. Feeling refreshed and peaceful, I was prepared for whatever the day held, feeling sure and attentive to whatever came my way. Emma and the kids were eating apples with peanut butter while watching The Lion King on the couch in the living room. While the kids were distracted, I quickly ran to my bathroom to take a quick shower after my run.

The week ended on a high note with a family outing to the local park, a special time that the twins and I looked forward to each Saturday. The park, a large area of greenery with tall trees and a well-equipped playground, was a perfect break from the routine of the past week.

When we arrived, the park was full of activity, families and children enjoying the sunny day. I found a spot near the playground where I could easily watch Evette follow behind Elijah, helping him as they both joined the other children. Evette supported Elijah as he used his gait trainer, pushing through the grass as I followed, settling onto a nearby bench with a satisfied smile.

I watched as Evette and Elijah took turns pushing each other on the swings. The sound of their laughter mixed with the other children's voices, creating a lively symphony of joy. My heart swelled with happiness, seeing them so carefree and spirited. Evette's hair flew behind her like a banner in the wind, while Elijah's focused face showed his determination to go a little higher with each push.

After a while, we moved on to the slides. I watched them climb the ladder, each step taken with eager anticipation. At the top, they paused, looked back to wave, and then slid down with joyful shouts, their faces lit up with excitement. Each time they reached the bottom, they would run back to the ladder, laughing and talking about who went fastest or made the funniest face on the way down.

As the afternoon went on, I gathered the twins for the next part of their outing—a picnic under one of the park's old oak trees. I spread a blanket on the grass, shaded by the tree's wide branches. The spot was peaceful, a little away from the busy playground, and offered a calm place for their meal.

I unpacked the picnic basket I had prepared earlier that morning. Inside were sandwiches neatly wrapped in wax paper, each filled with different ingredients to suit their tastes—from simple ham and cheese for Elijah to avocado and turkey for myself. Alongside the sandwiches, there were containers of fresh fruit salad, crispy vegetable sticks, and a few homemade cookies for a sweet treat.

As we ate, we shared stories about our favorite moments of the week. I listened intently as Evette spoke about her new interest in a science project we had done at home, and Elijah excitedly talked about building the highest tower with his blocks. I shared my highlights, including the joy of my morning walks and the progress of my personal projects.

This simple picnic under the old oak tree, with its gnarled branches casting intricate shadows on the ground, became a perfect moment of connection for us. We laughed, reminisced, and planned for the week ahead, our voices blending with the rustle of the leaves above.

As the sun started to go down, making long shadows in the park, I cleaned up our picnic stuff. We walked home from the park feeling happy and close, the simple fun of the day making our family stronger. Every time we went out like this, it reminded me how nice ordinary moments can be. I treasured these times, knowing they were what made our family ties strong, full of love and memories we shared.

THIRTEEN

On the morning of my baptism, I woke up early feeling excited, but also nervous. The sun was just beginning to peek through the bedroom window, casting a gentle glow on the curtains, blessing the day ahead. I had been preparing spiritually and mentally for this moment, and now it was finally here.

After putting on the soft blue dress I had chosen earlier in the week, I spent a quiet moment in prayer, asking for peace and clarity as I took this important step in my faith journey. I then kissed Evette and Elijah goodbye, promising to see them soon at the church with Aunt Emma.

Emma arrived just when I needed her, her car keys jingling as she walked in through the front door.

She quickly came over to me, opened her arms wide, and gave me a comforting hug.

"Don't worry about a thing, Evelyn," Emma said soothingly.

"I'll bring the kids over in time for the service. They're really excited to see their mom get baptized!" Emma's reassuring words and promise to take care of the kids for the day meant I could focus on my special moment without any extra stress.

Grateful for my sister's support, I gathered my things and a small Bible, my hands slightly trembling with anticipation. With one last look at my children, who were now happily chatting with Emma about the day ahead, I stepped out of the house.

The ride to the church was calm, with hardly any cars on the road early in the morning. When I parked and headed to the church, I knew exactly why I was there. I went in through the side door, and Pastor George was already there, waiting for me with a friendly smile that made me feel better.

"Good morning, Evelyn," Pastor George greeted me.

"We're all set up. Let's go over the process once more before everyone arrives."

The morning had been spent in a baptism class, where I learned more about the sacrament and began to prepare spiritually for the upcoming ceremony. The class left me feeling reflective and inspired, eager to embrace the commitments I would soon be making. When I was finished with Pastor George going over everything in the class about my baptism, I then followed him towards the baptismal pool, a centerpiece within the church that caught the eyes of all who entered. This pool was not just a simple basin; it was beautifully adorned with ornate tiles that made a pretty mosaic, giving it a sacred look. The tiles shimmered under the clear, cool water, which was filled just enough to reflect the light that streamed in through the church's windows. The effect was amazing, almost as if the water itself was alive with light and color, creating a calm and welcoming atmosphere for the baptism ceremony.

Placed at the front of the church, the baptismal pool was in clear view of every pew, making it a focal point for everyone. As the church filled with friends, family, and other community members, all eyes would be drawn to this spot where I would take this important step in my spiritual journey. The placement let everyone see the ceremony and symbolized the communal support and shared joy of this special moment in my faith.

Pastor George explained the steps of the ceremony. I would step down into the water, and he would say a few words about the meaning of baptism—how it symbolized washing away the old and starting a new life in Christ. Then, he would gently lower me back into the water, covering me entirely, before bringing me back up, symbolizing my rise to a new life.

As the pastor and I talked near the baptismal pool, I could hear the congregation arriving, making the church come alive. The doors opened and closed as people came in, bringing with them the sound of friendly chatter and greetings. The air was filled with laughter and soft conversations, creating a warm atmosphere of togetherness and expectation.

Standing beside the beautifully tiled pool, I took a deep breath to calm my nerves. Each breath made the moment feel more real. My heart beat fast with a mix of excitement and seriousness as I realized my baptism was about to happen. The significance of the ceremony weighed heavily on me, making me feel deeply connected to my spirituality.

Soon, the church began to quiet down as the service officially started. The organist played the first notes of a hymn, and soon, the air was filled with calm and uplifting music. The hymns, both familiar and reverent, floated through the church, setting a tone of reverence and reflection. The congregation joined in, their voices merging in harmony, filling the space with a spiritual warmth.

At this moment, Emma, along with Evette and Elijah, made their entrance. They walked down the aisle with eager steps and took their seats in the front row, in direct view of the baptismal pool. Their faces were bright with pride and joy, excited to see this important event in my life. Each of them wore expressions of support and happiness, eagerly taking part in the service and singing the hymns with enthusiasm.

I glanced over at my kids and sister. Their presence gave me comfort and encouragement. Seeing my loved ones gathered and smiling back at me made me feel confident and grateful. This support from family and friends made my baptism even more meaningful and memorable.

When it was time, I stepped into the baptismal pool. The water was cool against my skin, but my spirit felt warm. Pastor George stood beside me, his presence calming. He spoke about the journey of faith, then placed one hand on my back and the other on my arms.

"Evelyn, based on your confession of faith, I now baptize you in the name of the Father, the Son, and the Holy Spirit."

With that, he lowered me gently into the water.

The world went silent as the water covered me, a moment of deep solitude and reflection. Then, as I was raised back into the air, the sounds of the church returned—now cheering and clapping. My heart overflowed with joy as I stepped out of the pool, greeted by the smiling, tear-streaked faces of my children and sister.

The congregation came forward to offer hugs and words of congratulations. I felt renewed, not just by the water, but by the love and support of my community. My baptism was a declaration of my faith and an affirmation of my place within the church family, a moment of unity and celebration that I would cherish forever.

After the class, we made our way to a small, welcoming room next to the main sanctuary where we were scheduled to meet with Pastor Christopher. The room was bright, with sunlight streaming through large windows and children's artwork on the walls, giving it a cheerful, inviting atmosphere. As we entered, Pastor Christopher greeted us with a broad smile and a friendly wave.

"Hello, Evelyn, Evette, and Elijah! Welcome," he said, his voice warm and enthusiastic. His demeanor was gentle and friendly, with an ease that seemed to dissolve any nerves or hesitation the children might have felt. Evette looked up at him curiously, while Elijah clung a bit closer to me, watching Christopher with cautious interest.

Pastor Christopher invited them to sit at a round table with colorful placemats and a bowl of crayons in the center, designed to make young visitors feel at ease. He crouched down to Elijah's level and gave him a gentle smile.

"I hear you like puzzles," he said, remembering something I had mentioned in an email.
Elijah nodded, a small smile breaking through his shyness.

Once everyone was settled, Pastor Christopher explained the program, his voice full of excitement.

"We have many activities to help kids like Elijah grow and learn," he said.

"We have a sensory room with different textures and lights to help with sensory processing, and we organize games that encourage social interaction in a comfortable setting."

He then turned to Evette, who was already doodling on her placemat.

"And for you, Evette, we have art projects and creative writing workshops so you can express your creativity and stories," he added, showing her a portfolio of past projects done by other kids in the program.

I listened, my heart full of gratitude as I watched how Pastor Christopher talked to my children. He spoke directly to them, making them feel valued and understood. It was clear he had a real passion for helping children grow in confidence and ability. I felt reassured and was touched by the church's commitment to supporting families in all areas of their growth—spiritual, emotional, and developmental. I thanked Pastor Christopher for his time and the thoughtful planning that had gone into the program.

After discussing the program for children like Elijah and Evette, Pastor Christopher's expression softened. He leaned back slightly in his chair, his smile showing both pride and deep commitment.

"You know, Evelyn," he began, his voice gentle.

"This program isn't just my job; it's also very personal."

He paused, looking at a photo on his desk that I hadn't noticed before. It was a picture of a young boy with bright eyes and a joyful smile.

"This is my son, Lorenzo," Pastor Christopher said, his eyes lighting up as he said the name.

"He's the reason behind all of this. Lorenzo has Down syndrome, and from the day he was born, he showed me the beauty and potential of every person, no matter their abilities."

I listened closely, moved by his honest and open words. Pastor Christopher continued, sharing more about Lorenzo's life.

"When Lorenzo was younger, I saw how some programs didn't meet his needs or truly include him. It was hard, but it opened my eyes. I realized we could do so much more to help not just Lorenzo but all children, to include them in every part of life and learning."

His commitment to inclusion led him to start the program at the church, designed to support children of all abilities.

"It's about giving every child the help they need to succeed, to feel valued, and to be part of a community that celebrates their unique gifts," he explained. The program included many activities suited to different learning styles and needs, creating a place where children like Elijah and Lorenzo could learn and grow together.

I felt a surge of gratitude and admiration for Pastor Christopher. His personal connection to the program added depth to the conversation, making me even more sure about involving my children. It was clear the program was built on love and understanding—qualities I valued highly.

"Thank you for sharing that with me, Pastor Christopher," I said warmly.

"Lorenzo sounds like an amazing boy, and it's clear he inspires much of the wonderful work you do here."

Pastor Christopher nodded, a humble look on his face.

"He truly is," he replied.

"And I hope by sharing our story, it helps you see how committed we are here at Abundant Life Church to making a difference in the lives of all our children and families."

When I left, I felt confident about how the program could help my children and motivated by how sharing personal stories could bring people together. The church wasn't just a place to pray but also a center of community where my kids could get help and chances that fit them well. As we walked to the car under the shade of the old oak trees along the church driveway, I felt a new determination and hope about where our family was headed.

FOURTEEN

The kids and I drove home from the church, and Emma followed us in her car. The air felt warm and nice, perfect for a special family moment. The sun was setting, giving everything an orange glow. I still felt happy and excited about my baptism and couldn't wait to share everything with Emma, especially my chat with Pastor Christopher.

When we got home, we unloaded the car and settled inside. I turned to Emma and said,

"I met the Children's Youth Pastor after the service," I started, feeling excited.

"His name is Pastor Christopher, and he runs an awesome program for kids of all abilities."

Emma, who always made things fun, was driving through the quiet streets with me. I was smiling, ready for her to make me laugh. As we talked about the church, Emma saw a chance to tease me a bit, which she loved to do.

With a playful look, she turned to me and asked,

"Oh? Is Pastor Christopher handsome?" Her voice was teasing, trying to make me blush or smile.

This kind of joking was normal for Emma, always trying to make me laugh and feel relaxed. Her teasing wasn't just for fun; it was her way of showing she cared and making sure we could still find moments to laugh.

I chuckled, my cheeks turning red, not just from her question but from a joke she made weeks ago. We had talked about my wanting to find a new church, and Emma joked,

"Who knows, maybe you'll find a new husband there too!"

At the time, I laughed it off, but now, I found myself thinking about my meeting with Pastor Christopher.

"He's really kind, and yeah, he is quite handsome," I admitted, shaking my head at how silly this was.

"But more importantly, he's super passionate about what he does. He started the program because of his son, Lorenzo, who has Down syndrome. It's amazing to see someone so dedicated to helping all kids, not just his own."

Emma nodded, looking thoughtful as she listened to me talk about Pastor Christopher.

"That's wonderful, Evelyn. It sounds like the kids will really benefit from his program. And who knows? Maybe his dedication and kindness are just what you need right now."

I smiled, appreciating my sister's mix of humor and sincerity.

"Maybe," I said, thinking about the support I felt from the community at the church.

"It's just nice to meet someone who understands raising kids with special needs and turns it into something positive."

As the day wound down, Emma and I kept talking, sharing stories, and reflecting on our lives. Sitting comfortably in the living room, surrounded by the soft evening light, we exchanged stories and memories, both old and new. I felt so grateful for Emma's presence and support, not just today but always.

Our conversation flowed naturally, moving between serious talks about challenges and funnier exchanges that made us laugh. This balance showed the strong bond we shared, built on years of sisterhood with both happy and sad times.

As we talked, I appreciated Emma's thoughtful answers and insights that helped me see things differently, offering comfort when needed. Meanwhile, Emma's jokes and teasing lightened my heart, reminding me of the joy and fun in life.

The comfort and love between us filled the room, making it feel warm and safe. Moments like these were precious—times when talking with my sister could soothe my worries and lift my spirits, showing the strong support system we had in each other.

On a sunny Friday afternoon, with clear skies and a hint of the weekend ahead, I set out to the church to meet with Pastor Christopher. This wasn't just a regular visit; I was going to see the special needs center Pastor Christopher had told me about. As I drove, I felt both excited and a little nervous. I hoped this program would be perfect for Elijah and Evette, giving them the support they needed.

When I arrived, I parked my car and took a moment to calm myself before heading to the church's main entrance. My excitement grew with each step toward the large doors. Pastor Christopher was waiting for me as promised, standing under the shade of the awning. His presence was immediately comforting; he greeted me with a big, genuine smile.

"Welcome, Evelyn! I'm so glad you could join me today. Let's take a look around," he said warmly.

His friendly hello made me feel better as we walked into the church. Pastor Christopher's relaxed way of speaking made it easy to chat, and his welcoming gesture when he guided me showed that the tour was starting well. Inside, the cooler air felt nice after the heat outside, and I started to feel more hopeful about what I was going to see.

As we toured the center, I was impressed by the bright and welcoming environment. The walls were covered with colorful artwork and educational materials for kids of all abilities. Pastor Christopher showed me the different classrooms, each set up for various learning needs, and a sensory room filled with interactive experiences to help kids with sensory issues.

Even though the center was impressive, I still worried about Elijah fitting in. I told Pastor Christopher as we walked,

"I'm just a bit anxious about whether Elijah will truly be able to join in. He has some big delays, and

I'm afraid he might not blend in or get the attention he needs."

Pastor Christopher stopped and turned to me, looking serious but kind.

"Evelyn, I understand your concerns. But let me assure you, our program is all about inclusion. No matter the challenges a child faces, we are ready and committed to help them. We've set up our program to make sure every child, including Elijah, is not only included but also valued for their unique strengths."

He explained how the center worked.

"Our program is solely funded by donations, and we're lucky to have volunteer professionals—special education teachers and therapists—who work with us. They provide one-on-one support for any child who needs it, making sure all children can take part in every activity we offer."

As we continued the tour, Pastor Christopher led me to the outdoor area where the children's playground was. It was a bright and inviting space, clearly designed with care. He pointed out various pieces of playground equipment, each more impressive than the last.

He highlighted the accessible features, showing me the wide, smooth paths for wheelchair access and the specially designed swings for children with different physical abilities.

"This is just one example of how we make sure every child can join in the fun," he explained, his voice full of enthusiasm.

He gestured to a merry-go-round that was level with the ground, allowing children to easily roll on and off, making sure no child felt left out.

The thoughtful design of the playground showed the church's commitment to making sure all children could play and have fun, no matter their physical abilities. I listened, touched by the care and effort that had gone into making the space welcoming for everyone. It was clear from Pastor Christopher's words and the setup that the goal was to create a place where all children could play and explore without barriers, giving them the joy that every child deserves.

We ended our tour in a room where a small group of children were doing an art activity, closely watched and helped by a team of cheerful staff. Pastor Christopher introduced me to each staff member, who shared their experiences and the joys of working in such a supportive environment.

By the time my visit ended, I felt a deep relief and gratitude. What Pastor Christopher had shown me and the friendly atmosphere at the center helped calm my worries. As we got ready to say goodbye, I turned to Pastor Christopher and thanked him sincerely.

"Thank you so much for this, Pastor Christopher. Seeing everything and hearing about how the program works really makes me feel better. I feel much better about Elijah and Evette growing here," I said genuinely, my voice showing my gratitude.

Pastor Christopher responded warmly, his smile kind and encouraging.

"It's our pleasure, Evelyn," he assured me.

"We're here to support not just the children but their families too. We look forward to having Elijah and Evette join us and are excited to see them thrive."

His words reinforced the feeling of community and care that the center provided, strengthening my confidence in involving my children in the program. I left the center feeling not only relieved but also hopeful and inspired by the potential for my children in such a supportive setting.

As I drove back home through familiar streets, my mind was buzzing with thoughts of the visit. The drive gave me time to think about everything I had seen at the center, and my initial worries began to fade, replaced by a growing hope and excitement. The center was more than just a place; it was a lively community dedicated to nurturing and supporting all children.

I remembered how each space at the center was designed not just for learning and play but to create a sense of belonging and acceptance. The accessible equipment on the playground and the welcoming attitudes of everyone I met showed a strong commitment to including all children, no matter their abilities. It was clear to me that the center's goal was to help each child be their best self in an environment that celebrated their uniqueness.

This realization filled me with hopeful anticipation. I imagined Elijah and Evette thriving in such a supportive place, where they could make new friends, learn new things, and feel valued and understood. The drive home seemed shorter than usual as I thought about the possibilities and potential of enrolling my children in the center. By the time I reached home, I felt hopeful again about the future, sure that this community could be really important for the twins' growth and happiness.

FIFTEEN

After seeing the positive environment and strong support systems of the program, I felt assured and optimistic. It was clear that both Elijah and Evette could thrive there, embraced by a community that valued inclusion and personal growth.

Feeling relieved by my decision, I sat down at my kitchen table, the morning sunlight casting a warm glow across the room. I picked up the phone and dialed Pastor Christopher's number, the sound of the ringing mingling with the morning songs of birds outside my window.

"Pastor Christopher, it's Evelyn," I began, my voice steady and confident.

"I wanted to let you know that I've decided to enroll Elijah and Evette in the children's ministry program. After seeing everything and meeting the staff, I feel really positive about the support they will receive there."

Pastor Christopher's response was filled with warmth and enthusiasm.

"That's wonderful news, Evelyn! We're thrilled to have them join us. I'm confident that Elijah and Evette will benefit greatly from the activities and the community here. We'll make sure they feel right at home."

I thanked Pastor Christopher, feeling relieved and excited about the new opportunities ahead for my children at the center. As I said goodbye, I pictured Elijah and Evette fitting right into the program, learning new things, playing with their peers, and being part of a vibrant community. The image of my children happily engaged in fun and educational activities brought a smile to my face, filling me with optimism and joy.

When the call ended, I turned to share the uplifting news with Emma, who had just entered the room carrying a fresh pot of coffee, the aroma filling the air.

"It's official," I announced with a bright smile.

"The kids are going to be part of the children's ministry."

Emma quickly set the coffee pot down on the table, her face lighting up in response to my enthusiasm.

"That's fantastic, Evelyn! It's going to be so good for them, especially Elijah. I can't wait to see how they grow and change with all the new experiences," she replied, her voice filled with excitement. Her words echoed the feeling of hope I had, and we shared a happy moment, imagining the good things the program would do for my children.

The room was warm with the promise of fresh coffee and even fresher beginnings for Elijah and Evette. Both sisters looked forward to seeing the children thrive in an environment tailored to nurture and develop their skills, offering them a chance to discover new strengths and build lasting friendships. This was a step forward, a stride toward a brighter future for the entire family, and I felt deeply grateful for the support and the new paths unfolding before us.

We sipped our coffee, discussing the upcoming changes and the positive impact it would have on the children. The decision to involve Elijah and Evette in Pastor Christopher's program marked a new chapter in their lives, one filled with promise and the support of a community that understood and cherished every child's potential.

A month had passed since I decided to enroll Elijah and Evette in the children's ministry program at Abundant Life Church. As the weeks went by, I noticed positive changes in both of my children. Evette's confidence grew as she interacted more with her peers, joining activities with new enthusiasm and curiosity. The supportive and stimulating atmosphere of the program was nurturing her social skills and intellectual curiosity. But Elijah's progress stood out the most.

Previously somewhat reserved, Elijah began to show significant improvement in his communication and social interactions. I watched as my son started participating in group activities more actively, his initial hesitations giving way to eager involvement. His teachers reported that he was not only engaging more with the curriculum but also forming meaningful connections with other children, something that had been a challenge for him before.

These changes in Elijah were heartening. I saw a noticeable shift in his demeanor—a brightness in his eyes and a quickness to his smile that had been less frequent before. The structured, compassionate guidance provided by the children's ministry staff seemed to be exactly what he needed to unlock parts of himself that had been subdued. The program not only accommodated his special needs but celebrated his unique contributions, making him feel valued and included.

Each day as I picked up Elijah and Evette from Abundant Life Church, I was met with excited chatter about the day's activities and lessons. Their stories and shared experiences spoke volumes about their development and the nurturing impact of the program. For me, these observations confirmed that my decision to enroll them in the children's ministry was a pivotal step toward fostering their growth in a holistic and supportive environment.

I watched with a mix of pride and relief as Elijah began to thrive in the new environment. Before, he often struggled with new settings and routines, but the inclusive nature of the program and the careful, personalized attention he received made a big difference.

Each afternoon when I picked him up, I noticed that Elijah's usual restlessness had diminished. He greeted me with excited chatter about his day—about the sensory activities he enjoyed or the new friends he was making. His teachers had positive reports too. They shared stories of how Elijah had started to engage more during group activities, an area where he had once held back.

His sister Evette also blossomed in the program, but it was Elijah's transformation that truly stood out. Evette had always been more adaptable, but now she took on the role of a supportive sister with even greater zeal, often helping Elijah with transitions and pairing up with him during activities that require teamwork.

One sunny afternoon, as I sat on a bench near the playground watching Elijah play with other children, I realized how significant this change was. He was not only participating but also starting games, a sight that brought tears to my eyes. He was laughing, running, and calling out to other kids, fully a part of the joyful chaos around him.

The staff at the center, well-trained and compassionate, worked hard to integrate all kinds of therapeutic activities into every child's routine, ensuring that each child, especially those with special needs like Elijah, felt confident and included. Their way of doing things was kind yet worked well, creating a feeling of being part of a group and a community among the kids.

I felt deep gratitude toward Pastor Christopher and his team. Their commitment to creating an inclusive space where every child could thrive had opened a new world for Elijah, one where he could grow and learn at his own pace, surrounded by support and understanding.

As I prepared to leave the park with my children, I reflected on the past month. The decision to join the church's program had indeed been a turning point. Seeing Elijah's happy, engaged demeanor affirmed my belief in the power of a nurturing, inclusive community. I knew that as long as my children were supported in such a positive and adaptive environment, the future held endless possibilities for them.

As the holiday season approached, the church began to buzz with excitement and preparations for the annual Christmas musical, a cherished tradition at Abundant Life Church. It was a festive affair that brought together the entire congregation, featuring children from the Sunday school as the stars of the show. I was busy with the daily routines and uplifted by the positive changes in Elijah and hadn't given much thought to the upcoming event beyond planning to attend.

One chilly afternoon, as I picked up Elijah and Evette from the program, Mrs. Harper, the musical's director, and a Sunday school teacher, approached me with a beaming smile.

"Evelyn, I have some wonderful news," she exclaimed.

"Both Evette and Elijah have been given roles in the Christmas musical this year. We're thrilled to have them participate!"

I was taken aback, and pleasantly surprised by this unexpected development.

"Really? That's amazing! I had no idea they were interested," I responded as my heart swelled with pride.

"Yes," Mrs. Harper continued, her eyes twinkling with enthusiasm.

"They've been attending the rehearsals during our program hours, and both of them are doing wonderful. Elijah has a part in the choir, and he's been really enjoying the singing and the group practices. Evette has a small speaking role, and she's been practicing her lines with such dedication."

I thanked Mrs. Harper, as my mind raced with the delightful image of my children taking part in the musical. It was more than just an inclusion in an event; it was a testament to how the church community had embraced my family, recognizing and celebrating each child's abilities.

Over the next few weeks, I saw a new kind of excitement in Evette and Elijah. Evette often recited her lines at home, her voice clear and confident, while Elijah hummed the tunes of the Christmas carols, practicing whenever he got a chance. I helped them prepare, running lines with Evette and singing along with Elijah, turning their rehearsals into joyful family activities.

The night of the musical finally arrived, and the church hall was adorned with festive decorations, sparkling lights, and rows of poinsettias. The air was filled with the sweet scent of pine and the warm buzz of an expectant audience. As Emma accompanied me, we found our seats and scanned the stage for glimpses of Evette and Elijah.

As the curtains drew back, seeing Evette and Elijah, among their friends, in their costumes and beaming, made me incredibly happy. Elijah, standing tall with the choir, sang passionately, his voice harmonizing well with the others. Evette recited her lines gracefully, earning murmurs of praise from the crowd.

The show went off without a hitch, greeted with claps and cheers from the audience. I hugged my kids tightly afterward, feeling content, knowing this had not only highlighted their skills but also boosted their feeling of fitting in and accomplishment.

As the Christmas musical drew to a close, a gentle hush fell over the congregation, the air thick with anticipation for the final song. I was still beaming with pride from the performances so far and was completely unprepared for the announcement that came next. Mrs. Harper stepped forward, her voice warm and cheerful.

"For our final performance tonight, please welcome Evette and Elijah, who will sing a special duet of 'Jesus Loves Me.'"

My heart skipped a beat as I watched my children step confidently to the center of the stage. The piano began to play the soft, familiar melody, and as the first words were sung, a deep emotion swept through me. There they were, my children, standing together, their voices harmonizing in the quiet chapel.

Evette's voice was clear and sweet, perfectly complementing Elijah's, which carried a warmth that filled the room. As I watched my kids, I noticed a twinkle in Elijah's eye, a spark of joy and confidence that I had never seen so brightly before. It was a transformative moment for him, standing there on the stage, singing so beautifully. His usual hesitations, the challenges with his speech that often made him shy away from speaking up, seemed to vanish entirely under the soft stage lights.

Tears welled up in my eyes as I listened to their tender rendition of the song. Every note they sang seemed to resonate with the message of unconditional love and acceptance embodied by the lyrics. The congregation was deeply moved, some reaching for tissues, others smiling broadly at the touching scene.

Seeing Elijah and Evette perform together, supporting each other, and sharing such a special moment, I felt a surge of pride that was overwhelming. My heart was full, not just with pride, but with gratitude for the journey that had brought them to this point. My children, who had faced their unique challenges, were here, thriving and contributing their voices in such a meaningful way. The song concluded with a round of heartfelt applause, the audience standing to acknowledge the young performers. As Evette and Elijah took a bow, my applause was the loudest, my claps echoing my immense pride and joy.

That night, as the lights dimmed and the crowd began to disperse, I hugged my children tighter than ever before.

"You were both amazing," I whispered, my voice thick with emotion.

The memory of Elijah's twinkling eyes and the sound of their voices singing in perfect harmony would stay with me forever, a beautiful reminder of their growth and the love that surrounded them. This moment, under the glow of the stage lights, had shown me just how far my children had come, their spirits shining as brightly as the stars in the night sky.

That night, as I tucked a sleepy Elijah and Evette into bed, I reflected on the journey they had all undertaken since joining Pastor Christopher's program. The inclusion in the Christmas musical was more than just a festive participation; it was a symbol of the community's firm support and belief in every child's potential. This Christmas, I felt a deep gratitude for the gifts of inclusion, joy, and community spirit that Abundant Life Church had given my family.

SIXTEEN

As the applause settled and the last of the audience began to leave the chapel, my heart was still soaring from the children's performance. I saw Pastor Christopher near the stage, talking and laughing with some of the parents. Making my way through the dispersing crowd, I approached him with a grateful smile.

"Christopher, I can't thank you enough for what you've done for my kids," I said, my eyes reflecting the deep gratitude I felt.

Christopher turned to me, his face lit up with a sincere smile.

"It's truly been my pleasure, Evelyn. Seeing them tonight, how far they've come... it's why we do this," he responded warmly.

Moved by the moment and the evening's emotional performances, I hugged him, a spontaneous gesture of friendship and appreciation. Christopher returned the hug, and as we pulled back, he held onto my hands, looking into my eyes. The atmosphere was charged with a mix of emotions, and perhaps carried away by the intensity of the evening, Christopher acted impulsively.

Without thinking, he leaned in and kissed me. The kiss was brief but unexpected, and I was taken aback and instinctively pulled away. At that moment, a flicker of surprise and embarrassment crossed Christopher's face as he realized his mistake.

"I... I'm sorry, Evelyn. I didn't mean to overstep," he stammered, his cheeks flushed with a mix of regret and confusion.

I was still processing the sudden shift and managed a small smile to ease the tension.

"It's okay, Christopher," I said gently, trying to reassure him while still setting boundaries.

"I appreciate what you were feeling, but I think we should consider taking things slowly. Maybe we could start with a proper date, get to know each other outside of church and the children's program. I'm just not ready to jump into anything right now."

Christopher nodded, his expression understanding, yet visibly disappointed in himself for the misjudgment.

"You're right, Evelyn. I apologize for getting ahead of myself. A proper date sounds like a wonderful idea, whenever you feel ready."

The situation, though awkward, was handled with grace which allowed both of us to step back respectfully. I was touched by his quick apology and willingness to respect my wishes. We agreed to talk more later about potentially setting up a date, leaving the evening on a note of mutual respect and anticipation for what the future might hold.

As I walked back to my car, my mind was a whirl of emotions. The evening had been beautiful and uplifting because of the children's achievements, and now, with the possibility of exploring something new with Christopher, although cautiously, I felt both nervous and intrigued about what the future might bring.

Once outside, I guided Elijah and Evette toward the car, their spirits still high from the evening's excitement. As I buckled them into their seats, I noticed Emma approaching with a playful smirk on her face.

"So, I saw that little moment with Pastor Christopher," Emma teased, wiggling her eyebrows suggestively.
The lightness of her tone did little to alleviate the flush of embarrassment that rose in my cheeks.

I sighed, my eyes darting around the nearly empty parking lot as I wondered who else might have witnessed the moment.

"Emma, it was so embarrassing. I just pulled away from him right there in front of everyone. What if people saw? What are they going to think?" My voice was tinged with anxiety.

Emma's smile softened into a more sympathetic expression as she leaned against the car door, her tone reassuring.

"Hey, it's okay. These things happen. Honestly, I doubt many people noticed, and even if they did, it's not a big deal. You were surprised, that's all." Still, I couldn't shake off the humiliation.

"But what if it affects how people see me at church? Or what they would think of him?" I murmured, my worry evident.

Emma put a comforting arm around my shoulder.

"Look, Evelyn, the best way to clear the air is just to talk to him. Explain how you felt, why you reacted that way. I bet he's just as embarrassed, if not more. A conversation could help you both understand each other better." I nodded slowly, recognizing the wisdom in Emma's words.

"Maybe you're right. I should give him a call tomorrow. Clear things up before it becomes a bigger issue in my head."

Emma gave me a reassuring squeeze.

"Exactly! Plus, who knows? This could be a good chance to set things straight and maybe set up that proper date, on your terms. It doesn't have to be a big drama."

With my sister's encouragement, I felt a bit lighter, my earlier dread giving way to a resolve to handle the situation with maturity and openness. I thanked Emma for her support, grateful for having someone who could help put things in perspective.

As we drove home, the children chatted excitedly in the backseat about the musical, oblivious to my adult concerns. I smiled, hearing their happy laughter, and felt my thoughts becoming clearer.

Tomorrow, I plan to call Pastor Christopher. Whatever the outcome, I would handle it with grace, ensuring that both our feelings and roles within the church community remained respected and intact.

The following morning, after a restless night filled with mixed emotions, I decided it was best to address the situation head-on. I found a quiet moment after breakfast, once Elijah and Evette were settled with their morning activities. Taking a deep breath to steady my nerves, I picked up the phone and dialed Pastor Christopher's number. My heart thumped audibly as the phone rang, each tone echoing my apprehension.

"Hello, Evelyn," Pastor Christopher answered, his voice carrying a cautious warmth.

"Hi, Pastor Christopher," I began, my voice slightly shaky.

"I wanted to talk about last night... after the musical."
There was a brief pause on the line, a silence that spoke volumes.

"Yes, I've been thinking about that too," Christopher replied, his tone serious but gentle.

"I'm really sorry if I made you uncomfortable. It wasn't my intention." I appreciated his immediate apology, which eased some of my tension.

"Thank you for saying that, Christopher. I was taken by surprise, and I didn't know how to react at that moment," I admitted.

"I understand, and I regret that it happened in such a public setting. It wasn't fair to you," he continued, his sincerity clear.

"I value our friendship and what you've brought to the church, especially with the kids' program. I hope this doesn't change things between us."

I listened, feeling a mixture of relief and respect for his honest approach.

"I'm glad we can talk about it like this. I do value our friendship too, and I'm hopeful we can move past this. I wasn't ready for a kiss, especially not like that and not yet," I explained, finding strength in my clarity.

Christopher's response was understanding.

"I respect that, Evelyn. And I'd like to make it up to you, if you're willing. Maybe we could start over, perhaps with that proper date you mentioned? Just a casual coffee, as friends, to regain some normalcy?"

I considered his proposal, weighing my readiness to step forward.

"I think I'd like that," I decided, a smile beginning to form as the tension dissipated.

"A coffee as friends could be a good way for us to reconnect and ensure we're both comfortable with where things stand."

"That sounds perfect. I'll make sure it's relaxed, no expectations. Just two friends spending some time together," Christopher agreed, a note of relief in his voice.

As we set a time for our coffee meeting, I felt a genuine sense of closure and a way to mend and possibly deepen our friendship under clearer terms. Just before we ended the call, Pastor Christopher spoke up,

"Hey Evelyn, you can just call me Chris."

Hanging up the phone, I felt reassured. I navigated a delicate conversation with grace and honesty, ensuring my feelings were respected while maintaining the friendship that was important to me and beneficial for the church community. With the conversation behind me, I felt ready to focus on the day ahead, content that Christopher and I could continue to work together and have mutual respect and understanding.

Several days after our phone conversation, the morning of the coffee date arrived. I felt a flutter of nervous excitement as I prepared for the outing.

Choosing a casual yet neat outfit, I reflected on the conversation we had, feeling positive about setting a new foundation for our friendship.

The café we picked was a cute place known for its warm feel and great coffee. It was on the corner of the main street, with bright flowers by the door and the soft sound of quiet talks and clinking coffee cups inside. Christopher was already there when I arrived. He was standing by the door with a warm smile and waved me over as I walked up to him, giving off a relaxed demeanor that helped to ease my initial nerves.

"Hi, Evelyn. I'm glad you could make it," he said, his tone friendly and genuine.

"Hi, Christopher. It's a lovely place," I replied, admiring the charming interior. We chose a small table by the window, where the morning light spilled across the wooden surface, casting playful shadows.

As we sat, a waiter quickly attended to us, and we ordered our coffees—simple and straightforward, just like the intent of our meeting. With the order placed, the initial formalities gave way to a more relaxed conversation.

"So, how have the kids been since the musical?" Christopher asked, clearly keen to keep the topics light and personal but not too intimate.

"They've been great, really buzzing from the experience. Evette has been asking about the next event she can participate in," I shared, my face lighting up as I talked about my children.

"That's wonderful to hear," Christopher responded, his interest evident. He shared a bit about the plans for the church's upcoming events, ensuring that the kids would be and feel included.

As our coffees arrived, steaming and aromatic, the conversation gently shifted to more general topics—favorite books, movies, and even some talk about the community projects Christopher was passionate about. I found myself enjoying the chat, appreciating the opportunity to learn more about Christopher in a setting that was free of any previous awkwardness.

"I've been thinking of getting more involved with some community outreach programs," I mentioned, stirring my coffee thoughtfully.

"That sounds fantastic," Christopher said, his eyes bright with encouragement.

"There's always something going on, and extra hands are always needed. Plus, I think you'd bring a lot of great ideas."

The time passed pleasantly, with both of us comfortable in the casual flow of conversation. It was clear that our previous interaction hadn't ruined our ability to communicate and enjoy each other's company.

As we wrapped up our conversation and got ready to go, I felt proud of what we accomplished. The coffee date had served its purpose—restoring our friendship to a comfortable place and opening doors for future cooperation and friendship.

"Thank you for this, Christopher. It was really nice just to sit and talk," I said, standing by the door.

"Thank you, Evelyn. Let's make sure to do this again, maybe make it a regular thing," Christopher suggested with a hopeful smile. I nodded in agreement, pleased with the suggestion.

"I'd like that," I said, stepping out into the sunlight, feeling content and optimistic about the future of our friendship.

Following the success of our casual coffee meeting, Christopher decided to invite me out for a more formal evening. He chose a well-regarded restaurant in town known for its elegant atmosphere and exquisite cuisine, hoping to create a memorable evening for both of us.

On the day of the date, I asked Emma to watch the twins, explaining that I was going out for the evening. Emma, ever the supportive sister, agreed immediately, insisting that I deserved a nice night out.

"Go have fun, and don't worry about a thing here," Emma encouraged me, smiling.

I dressed carefully for the occasion, choosing a simple yet elegant dress that made me feel both beautiful and comfortable. Christopher arrived to pick me up right on time, looking sharp in a well-fitted suit. He greeted me with a warm, appreciative smile that set the tone for a promising evening.

The restaurant we arrived at was softly lit, with gentle music playing in the background and tables draped in fine linen. The ambiance was sophisticated yet welcoming. We were seated at a quiet table with a view of the restaurant's small, tastefully landscaped garden.

As we looked over the menu, we chatted about light topics, sharing laughs and enjoying the relaxed setting. We ordered our meals, choosing dishes recommended by our attentive waiter. I opted for seafood pasta, while Christopher decided on a steak, both accompanied by a glass of wine. The food, when it arrived, was delicious—perfectly cooked and beautifully presented, enhancing the overall experience of our elegant evening.

Throughout the dinner, their conversation deepened, touching on personal goals, past experiences, and future dreams. I found myself opening up more than I had expected, comforted by Christopher's genuine interest and respectful attentiveness.

After sharing a decadent chocolate cake for dessert, the night gradually came to an end. Christopher drove me home, both of us expressing how much we had enjoyed the evening. Standing at my doorstep, I felt a mix of contentment and anticipation.

"Thank you for a wonderful evening, Christopher. It was really special," I said, my smile reflecting my words.

Christopher nodded, his eyes showing he felt the same.

"I'm glad you enjoyed it, Evelyn. I hope we can do this again soon," he replied, sounding hopeful. The night ended with a friendly hug, and a perfect, respectful close to our date. The evening had surpassed my expectations, and I was pleased with the pace and natural progression of my growing relationship with Christopher.

After returning home from my elegant date with Christopher, I quietly checked in on Elijah and Evette. They were sound asleep, tucked in, and peaceful. A feeling of relief and warmth washed over me. Satisfied that my children were well and resting, I made my way back down the hall.

Emma was waiting for me in the living room, her expression curious and eager.

"So, how did it go?" She asked, her voice full of excitement. I smiled, feeling a swirl of emotions just before I recounted the night. I went to the kitchen, poured myself a glass of wine, and joined Emma on the couch.

"It was really wonderful," I began, my eyes sparkling with the joy of the evening.

"The restaurant was beautiful, the food was delicious, and the conversation... it was just so easy and meaningful."

Emma listened intently as I offered details about every part of the evening—from the way Christopher had chosen a restaurant with a quiet, romantic ambiance to our shared dessert and the laughs we exchanged.

"He was so thoughtful throughout the whole evening, really making sure I was comfortable and enjoying myself," I added, my voice softening.

"And...?" Emma prodded, sensing there was more to the story.

My cheeks flushed slightly with a happy blush.

"And, we ended the night with a kiss. This time, it felt right. It was gentle, respectful... and very much wanted," I confessed, my smile broadening.

Emma squealed lightly, delighted for me.

"That sounds perfect, Evelyn! I'm so happy for you. It sounds like things are really starting to look up with Christopher."

Emma and I continued to chat as I expressed my hopes and some of my cautious optimism.

"I think we're taking things at a good pace. Tonight felt like a real step forward in getting to know each other better," I mused, sipping my wine. Emma nodded, her expression supportive.

"Just take it one step at a time. It's important that you're comfortable and happy. But from what you're telling me, it sounds like you both are on the same page, which is great!"

As our conversation wound down, a thoughtful expression shadowed my face.

"Christopher is really charming," I mused, swirling the wine in my glass. A flicker of doubt crossed my face as I recalled my past.

"You know, Michael was charming too, at the beginning." Emma noticed the change in my demeanor and leaned forward, her expression earnest.

"I know you're worried, but Christopher is nothing like Michael," she reassured me firmly, wanting to ease any doubts.

I looked at her with a mix of hope and hesitation in my eyes.

"Think about it, Evelyn," Emma continued, her voice gentle yet confident.

"Christopher has been consistently kind and respectful, not just to you but to everyone in the community. He's involved, he genuinely cares about helping people, and he's dedicated to his work with the kids. And remember how he handled the situation after the kiss? He was apologetic and respectful of your feelings."

I nodded, listening intently as Emma laid out the differences, each point helping to ease my concerns.

"Plus, he's open and honest with you. He doesn't just show up with charm; he supports it with real actions. That's not what we saw with Michael. Michael was all about grand gestures at first, but he lacked the consistency and the depth that Christopher shows," Emma added, her voice filled with sincerity.

I took a deep breath, the weight of my sister's words sinking in.

"You're right," I admitted, a small smile returning to my face.

"Christopher has been nothing but considerate and transparent. And tonight just proved how thoughtful he can be."

Emma smiled back, happy to see me feeling reassured.

"Exactly. Just give it some time and keep communicating. I think you'll find that Christopher's actions will consistently show his true character."

Feeling comforted by Emma's perspective, my doubts started to disappear. I was grateful for my sister's insight, helping me see the situation more clearly and differentiate between past hurts and present possibilities. With a happier heart and a clearer mind, I finished my wine, ready to face whatever came next with fresh hope and trust.

As we wrapped up our conversation, I felt content. Sharing the details with Emma not only allowed me to relive the pleasant memories but also helped me process my feelings about moving forward. With a heart full of budding emotions and the quiet support of my sister, I felt ready to see where this new relationship could lead, embracing the possibilities with an open heart. Reflecting on the night as I prepared for bed, I felt grateful for the new chapter unfolding in my life, filled with new experiences and possibilities.

SEVENTEEN

After Emma left for the night, I found myself alone with my thoughts, reflecting deeply on our conversation. I poured myself another small glass of wine and settled into the quiet of the evening. My mind wandered back to the early days with Michael. Those days had been filled with charm and promise, like a fairy tale. Michael had swept me off my feet and given me a beautiful, dreamlike wedding—a day that seemed perfect in every way.

As I sipped my wine, I remembered how I had been captivated by the romance and grand gestures. The wedding was everything I had hoped for, decorated with flowers, laughter, and dances under a starlit sky. It was a day straight out of a storybook, where I felt like a princess in a beautiful gown, surrounded by friends and family, celebrating love.

However, as the months and years passed, I realized that a wedding day is just a day, and a marriage is made up of all the days that come after. The charm that Michael initially displayed faded as the realities of daily life set in. What I had truly wanted was not just a fairy tale wedding, but a fairy tale marriage—one filled with love, respect, and partnership every day, not just on special occasions.

Sitting there in the stillness, I acknowledged to myself that what I had experienced with Michael was the excitement of a beginning, not the steadfastness of a lifelong journey. The difference between that relationship and what I was beginning to build with Christopher became even clearer. Christopher's kindness wasn't just surface-level charm; it was deep and consistent, visible in his actions and how he treated everyone around him, including me and my children.

I realized that with Christopher, the potential for a true partnership existed—one based on mutual respect and shared values, not just initial attraction and grand events. This thought comforted me, and slowly, I began to feel more hopeful about opening my heart again, this time with a better understanding of what real, enduring love could look like.

As I sat calmly, swirling the last sips of wine in my glass, I let myself think quietly for a moment. The soft sound of the evening surrounded me, making me feel calm and thoughtful. The wine had been comforting, and as I set the empty glass aside, I felt a real feeling of calmness wash over me.

In the stillness, I considered the future. It was a path not yet taken, filled with uncertainties and the promise of new beginnings. I knew that moving forward would not just require changes on the outside—new places, new faces—but also openness and trust from within. It would mean letting go of past hurts and embracing potential, no matter how vulnerable that might make me feel.

Yet, as I thought about what lay ahead, I felt a surge of readiness. I was prepared to explore these new possibilities, to give myself over to the hope of finding the kind of deep, fulfilling connection I had always yearned for. The idea of a fairy tale marriage, not one of fantasy but of real, enduring love and partnership, seemed within reach. This wasn't about recapturing what was lost but about rediscovering the capacity for joy and commitment in a relationship built on mutual respect and understanding.

This moment of introspection reaffirmed my resolve. I felt more equipped than ever to face whatever challenges came next, with a heart open to giving and receiving love in its fullest measure. I was ready to take the steps necessary to build the life and the love I had always dreamed of, trusting in my strength and the journey ahead to lead me to a place of lasting happiness.

I longed for a partner who would love my children as unconditionally as I did. This was a deep desire in my heart, something I knew was essential for any lasting relationship I would enter. However, this wasn't what I experienced with Michael. Despite the charm and the enchanting start to our relationship, Michael's affection towards my children was, at best, inconsistent.

As I sat reflecting in the quiet of my home, I thought back to how Michael interacted with Elijah and Evette. It became clear over time that his interest and patience were fleeting. He rarely engaged in their activities or took the time to truly understand their needs. His attention often seemed forced, lacking the genuine warmth and acceptance that I knew my children deserved.

This realization struck me deeply, leaving a lasting impression that was both painful and transformative. I vividly remembered the internal conflict that had gripped me during those tumultuous times—the tug-of-war between my lingering affection for Michael and my powerful instinct to protect my children's emotional well-being. This struggle was more than just a fleeting concern; it was a profound dilemma that weighed heavily on my heart each day.

The gravity of deciding the future of my relationship with Michael while ensuring the happiness and security of my children was immense. It put me in an almost constant state of introspection and uncertainty, making me reevaluate what I truly wanted and what was best for my family. Every interaction, every decision, seemed to pull me in opposing directions, and the burden of this emotional strain was palpable.

I often found myself lying awake at night, the quiet hours bringing no relief but instead a flood of thoughts about what was right and what was necessary. It was a time marked by deep soul-searching, where my responsibilities as a mother clashed with my desires as a partner. This internal battle forced me to question the viability of my relationship with Michael, making me confront painful truths about love, loyalty, and personal happiness.

Eventually, I realized that my primary role was to protect and nurture my children. This understanding became the guiding principle in my decisions. It led me to a path of tough choices, where clarity about what needed to be done gradually overshadowed the confusion and pain of the past. My journey through this emotional landscape was difficult, but it was necessary for me to see a future that held promise not just for me, but for my children as well.

In contrast, as I now thought about my growing relationship with Christopher, I saw a different picture. Christopher's approach to my children was filled with genuine care and inclusiveness. His actions showed a man who not only respected me as a person but also valued me as a mother. He interacted with Elijah and Evette with a kind-heartedness and patience that never seemed to waver, treating them with the same respect and kindness he showed me.

This difference was clear and important. It showed what was truly important to me—a partner who not only loved me but also embraced my children with open arms and an open heart. It gave me hope and a clearer vision of what I wanted in a relationship, reinforcing my belief that my children's happiness and acceptance were non-negotiable in my search for love and companionship.

As I considered the growing closeness between myself and Christopher, a flicker of hesitation held me back from fully embracing the idea of taking our friendship to the next level. This hesitation was rooted in my past experiences, especially how things had unfolded with Michael. Despite the evident differences between Michael and Christopher, the shadows of my previous relationship loomed large, casting a shadow of doubt over my current feelings.

Sitting quietly one evening, I thought about these things. I appreciated Christopher's kindness and the genuine affection he showed towards me and my children. His consistent care and understanding contrasted sharply with my past, offering a hopeful glimpse of a different kind of partnership. Yet, the fear of repeating old mistakes—of misjudging kindness for lasting commitment—nagged at me.

I worried about the impact a new relationship could have on my children if things didn't work out. The thought of introducing them to a significant person in my life only to face the possibility of another separation made me cautious. I knew how resilient Elijah and Evette were, but I also knew my primary role was to protect their hearts as well as my own.

Additionally, there was the challenge of blending our lives fully. While Christopher had been nothing but supportive, I understood that building a life together would involve navigating the complexities of integrating our families, schedules, and expectations. The practicalities of such a union were daunting, and I wondered if we were both prepared for the potential adjustments and compromises.

These considerations made me pause. I cherished the friendship and the emerging feelings I had for Christopher, but I also recognized the need for more time. Time to understand my own heart, to evaluate the depth of our connection, and to ensure that moving forward would enrich not just my life, but the lives of my children too. I resolved to proceed with patience and open communication, trusting that if our bond was meant to deepen, it would do so at a pace that felt right for everyone involved.

I sat quietly, the silence of the evening settling around me as I pondered my feelings. The more I thought about it, the clearer it became that fear was the root of my hesitation. Fear of repeating past mistakes, fear of exposing my children to potential heartache, and fear of stepping into the unknown with Christopher. These fears clouded my heart, making it difficult to move forward.

But as I considered these fears, a strong resolve began to form within me. I had always been a woman of faith, and it was in moments like these that I turned to prayer for guidance and strength. I didn't want to let fear dictate my life's choices or hinder the potential happiness that seemed just within reach.

So, I found a quiet spot in my home, where the calmness could surround me, and I prayed. I poured out my heart, seeking clarity and peace. I asked for the wisdom to distinguish between genuine caution and unnecessary fear, and for the courage to make choices that would lead to true happiness for me and my children.

As I prayed, a calm feeling came over me. I felt a gentle reassurance that I was not alone in my journey. My faith had always guided me through the toughest times, and I trusted that it would not fail me now or in the future. With a renewed spirit, I decided that I would keep my faith and not let fear win.

I decided to approach my relationship with Christopher with an open heart and mind, ready to see where our growing connection might lead. I felt strong enough to face whatever came next, comforted by the belief that, no matter the outcome, I was making choices based on faith, not fear. This decision brought a sense of freedom, and I felt ready to embrace the possibilities that awaited me with confidence and hope.

Once I chose to prioritize my faith over my fears, there was a noticeable change in how I viewed the world around me. It was like I had removed a filter that had long clouded my vision, allowing me to see my surroundings with newfound clarity and appreciation. This shift in perspective was profound, revealing the richness of my everyday life that I had previously overlooked.

With this new way of seeing, even the smallest details began to stand out clearly. The gentle way the morning light spilled across the breakfast table, the laughter of my children echoing from another room, and the comforting rhythm of my daily routines all took on special significance. These moments and details had always been there, but I had been too preoccupied with worries and uncertainties to truly notice them.

This new understanding brought a feeling of amazement and thankfulness. I found myself pausing more often, taking in the simple beauty of a blooming flower in my garden or the intricate dance of shadows and light in my living room as the day shifted into the evening. Each observation was like a small gift, a reminder of the beauty of the present moment that fear had once hidden from me.

By placing my faith above my fears, I not only changed my internal feelings but also transformed how I engaged with the world around me. This shift helped me appreciate the here and now, encouraging a mindfulness that enriched my daily experiences. It was as though by choosing faith, I had opened a door to a world filled with color, beauty, and tranquility that had always been there, waiting to be acknowledged and cherished.

As I spent my days with Evette and Elijah, I started to appreciate the laughter and love that filled our home more deeply. I noticed how Evette's eyes sparkled with curiosity and intelligence as she tackled her homeschool lessons or created imaginative stories. I saw the strength and resilience in Elijah, watching him navigate his challenges with a quiet determination that inspired me every day.

At church and in our community, I had a feeling of belonging that I hadn't felt before. I observed the genuine connections forming between my family and others, including the nurturing environment that Pastor Christopher and his program provided. It wasn't just the activities themselves but the inclusiveness and acceptance we experienced that made me realize we were exactly where we needed to be.

This newfound appreciation extended to my personal growth. I recognized the strides I had made in overcoming my past, my development in faith, and my courage in facing my fears. The help from Emma, the kindness from Christopher, and the community we found at the church all added to a feeling of being whole and happy in my life.

In these moments of clarity, I understood that my decision to trust in my faith and push past my fears was the right one. I, along with Evette and Elijah, were indeed where we were supposed to be—surrounded by love, supported through faith, and thriving in our own unique ways. This realization filled me with a profound peace, affirming my faith-driven choice to embrace life's possibilities.

EIGHTEEN

As the seasons changed from the cold of winter to the blooming of spring and then to the warmth of summer, my relationship with Christopher grew. Every month, our bond got stronger, filled with many shared moments that brought joy and support. We learned to handle life's small problems together, finding comfort in each other's views and strength in our teamwork.

We understood each other better through long talks that lasted into the night, quiet times together, and laughing over inside jokes that became our special way of communicating. These moments were not just happy times but also the threads that made our relationship strong and lasting.

Christopher's son, Lorenzo, also became a big part of this growing family. His special bond with me showed in the way his eyes lit up when I entered a room or how excitedly he shared his day's adventures with me. I treated Lorenzo with the same love and patience I showed my kids, creating a caring space that encouraged him to be himself.

Similarly, my kids welcomed Christopher into their lives. His gentle guidance and fun-loving nature made him a favorite playmate and a trusted adult they could rely on. The mutual affection shown in our family outings became the highlights of our days. Whether it was a visit to the zoo, a picnic by the lake, or a movie night at home, these outings made us feel like a united family.

These outings were not just fun but also chances for all of us to contribute to our shared family life, making our bonds stronger. Each outing, each shared laugh, and each moment of understanding built a foundation of a blended family filled with love, respect, and joy. This collective happiness was clear and made us feel warm and secure.

As the year went on and the leaves started to turn bright autumn colors, it became clear that what Christopher and I had was very special. Our relationship, built on deep emotional connection and mutual support, had grown to include our families, creating a blended circle filled with love and laughter.

One cool autumn evening, as the air turned chilly and leaves colored the scenery in shades of yellow and brown, Christopher and I reflected on the year we had spent together. It was a year filled with laughter, shared dreams, and growing closeness. It was then that Christopher decided it was the perfect time to take our relationship to the next level. He knew in his heart that he wanted to spend his future with me, blending our lives and families into one, and I felt the same.

To show his feelings and intentions, Christopher carefully planned a special day for us, designed to revisit the important moments of our relationship and celebrate the memories we had created together. He chose places that held significant meaning for us, each place a chapter in our story.

The day was to start at the local art museum where we had first felt our deep connection over long, thoughtful walks among the paintings hanging on the wall. It was here, among the peaceful beauty of creativity, that we had opened up about our pasts, our hopes for the future, and our beliefs, discovering how closely our values and dreams matched.

From there, Christopher wanted to take me to the coffee shop where we had spent many afternoons, sitting in our favorite corner booth, sipping lattes and having conversations that made the world feel like it stood still. This spot had become a special place for us, a place where we could escape our daily routines and just be together, often losing track of time as we talked.

Next, we took a walk along the riverside pathway where we shared a kiss under the starlit sky. The gravel path, with the flowing sounds of the river and giant trees with their rustling leaves, is when I witnessed the moment our relationship changed from friendship to something deeper, marked by a spontaneous, tender kiss that said so much.

Once we left the riverside, Christopher planned to end the day at a special overlook that offered a beautiful view of the city. It was there, during a sunset early in our relationship, that we had made wishes for the future, tossing coins into a small wishing well, laughing and hoping about the possibilities ahead.

A few weeks later, Christopher had asked me out on another date, a picnic in the park. But this time was a little different. He said he had a special surprise for me and I would see it waiting for me at the park. He instructed me to go to the park across the street from the church. Intrigued, I got dressed and was about to call Emma to watch the kids, but just as I picked up the phone to dial her number, there was a knock at the door. I walked into the foyer and noticed Emma standing on the other side of my front door.

"I was just about to call you."
I told her as I turned to grab the broom to reach my other missing shoe that was somehow kicked underneath the cabinet that held all of my fine china. As I pulled the shoe out and picked it up to put it on, Emma stated,

"Well, here I am, and at your service. I guess you have a date." She said with a knowing smirk. How did she even know? I thought.

I walked back to my bedroom to finish getting ready and start doing my make-up. I put on a little eyeliner, mascara, and a thin layer of lip gloss before throwing them back in my make-up bag. I then plugged in my curling iron and waited for it to get hot. While I was waiting, I walked into the living room to find Emma and the kids getting dressed in new clothes that Emma bought them.

"A little too nice to play outside, don't you think?" I asked, looking at Emma curiously.

She looked back at me and shrugged her shoulders. I could tell she was up to something, but I didn't know what.

I couldn't help but shake my head at her. She was never a good liar. It was clear she had planned to take them out, which was fine with me. I didn't think she needed to keep the kids in the house anytime I left to go somewhere, but it was that they were dressed in attire that didn't fit the idea of a playground.

I turned around, making my way back to the bathroom to check if the curling iron was hot yet. That thing was so old, I don't know how it still worked. But, it did, and I was going to use it until the day it didn't anymore. I parted my hair, pulling out medium-sized chunks to begin curling. My hair was long and wavy, but it wasn't wavy enough to give it the curl I wanted. The only way I could do that was several passes with the curling iron and a ton of hairspray. Section by section, and about forty-five minutes later, my hair was done. I sprayed a heavy amount of hairspray, enough that would probably suffocate someone if they didn't have good enough ventilation.

I looked at myself in the mirror and was finally happy with the look. My hair fell perfectly just over my left eye, and the curls were beautiful all around. I was proud of the masterpiece I had created atop my head. After unplugging the curler, and putting away the hair spray, I walked out of the bathroom, and into the living room.

"How do I look?" I asked, lightly swinging my hair from side to side.

"Mommy!" Evette shouted with excitement.

Elijah's silent stares at me filled my heart as he wore the cutest smile. I wrapped my arms around Evette and then Elijah. I explained where I was going and that I would see them later. Elijah's smile still never left his face. I hugged Emma and thanked her again for watching the kids while I was gone.

I picked up my purse, grabbed my keys off the hook and my phone, and walked out the door. I got into the car and pulled out of the driveway. It took about fifteen minutes to get to the park by the church and I hoped Christopher wasn't waiting too long.

When I arrived at the park, I found Christopher standing in the middle of the field next to a blanket spread out across the grass. There was a cooler, a couple of wine glasses, and a small bowl filled with grapes, strawberries, and pineapple. It was the cutest setup, and I could feel the butterflies in my stomach.

I greeted him with a soft kiss, and we sat down on the blanket. Christopher popped open the bottle of wine and began to pour a glass and handed it to me. I just so happened to notice as I took the first sip that the cooler was still open and I peeked inside, noticing more wine glasses and a bottle of sparkling grape juice, next to a bag of ice which had me puzzled. Before I could ask him what the other glasses were for, I noticed Emma walking toward us with Evette, Elijah, and Lorenzo following behind.

As Emma and the kids approached us Christopher stood up and gently took my hands in his. I knew what was coming next, and I was thrilled. Trying to keep my composure, I let him give his speech.

His gaze was soft, his face serious, and in that quiet park, under the big oak tree, it felt like the world paused around us.

Christopher's voice, when he started to speak, was steady but full of emotion.

"Evelyn," he began, gently rubbing my hands with his thumbs,

"This past year with you has been the happiest of my life. You and your children have brought so much joy into our lives."

His voice softened even more as he continued, and his sincerity was clear.

"I see a future for us, one filled with love, family, and faith. A future where we keep supporting and caring for each other."

He paused, looking into my eyes, making sure I felt each word.

"You've shown me what it means to love with patience and kindness, and every day with you proves the strength of a true partnership. Your compassion, your strength, your commitment to your family inspire me every day."

Christopher's words were not just about his feelings but a promise of commitment, a vision of a future where we could grow together, facing life's challenges with shared strength and joy.

"With you, I feel we can face anything, knowing that as long as we're together, we'll turn challenges into opportunities. I want to keep building this life with you, to be a partner to you, and a father to Evette and Elijah, just as I am to Lorenzo."

His words hung in the air, filled with emotion and promise, as the gentle breeze moved the leaves above them, casting light shadows on the blanket where they sat. The setting, the words, and the deep feelings we shared created a moment of strong closeness and connection, showing all they had built together and all they hoped to build in the future.

Christopher's heartfelt words lingered in my heart, a clear sign of his deep feelings. He paused and glanced at Lorenzo and Elijah, who stood a little distance away with excited, eager faces. They knew this moment was important and understood their roles, taking it seriously. With a nod from Christopher, the boys stepped forward, holding a small, velvet box. Christopher took the box from them with a thankful smile, then turned back to me. He moved slowly and carefully, lowering himself to one knee on the soft grass under the old oak tree. This simple, traditional act made me catch my breath. The autumn leaves created a colorful scene around us, and even nature seemed to stop in respect for the moment. When he opened the box, it showed a simple but beautiful ring. The design was plain but elegant, fitting my taste perfectly. The light sparkled on the diamond, creating tiny rainbows around us and matching the light in Christopher's eyes.

Holding the ring, his voice softened, but every word was full of meaning.

"Evelyn," he began, looking right at me,

"Will you marry me? Will you let me be part of your and your children's life, not just today, but every day forward?"

His question was simple but very deep, full of hope and honesty.

His proposal wasn't just about marriage. It was about becoming a permanent part of my life, sharing in all the joys and challenges, the small moments and the big ones. It was a promise to be there for me, Evette, and Elijah, to be a loving and supportive presence.

As Christopher knelt there with the ring, the park seemed to hold its breath, waiting for my answer. The children watched quietly, their faces showing a mix of nervousness and joy. They knew how important this moment was. Under the oak tree, with the fall colors around us and the future ahead, everything seemed to come together into one beautiful possibility.

I felt a surge of emotions, tears filled my eyes, showing just how much this moment meant. The park, with its rustling leaves and gentle breeze, seemed to stop, quietly watching the tender scene under the old oak tree.

I looked at the children—Lorenzo, Evette, and Elijah—who watched with wide, hopeful eyes. Their faces glowed with happiness, reminding me how much this meant to our whole family. Seeing them so eager and full of love made the moment even more special.

Looking back at Christopher, I saw more than just my partner. I saw someone who had always shown deep respect and unconditional love, not just for me but for my children too. In his eyes, I saw our past and the promise of our future—a future where we could keep growing, face challenges, and enjoy happy moments together.

I thought about our journey, the early uncertainties, the deep talks that had helped us understand each other, and the shared moments that had become part of our lives. Christopher had been there through it all, always supportive and strong.

Feeling the importance of my decision, I reached out, my hands shaking a little, to touch the ring. It was more than just a symbol of engagement; it was a promise, a commitment to walk through life together, no matter what.

"Yes, Christopher," I whispered, my voice full of emotion, barely louder than the rustling leaves.

"Yes, I will marry you."
My words were a soft echo, a gentle affirmation of our love and partnership. As a tear ran down my cheek, I felt calm and sure. The challenges we had faced, the growth we had shared—all of it had led us to this beautiful, defining moment.

The children cheered excitedly, their voices blending with the rustling leaves in the breeze. Christopher stood up, his face glowing with joy. He hugged me warmly, and the children crowded around us, sharing in the happiness of our engagement. Under the oak tree, surrounded by nature and family, we celebrated the start of a new chapter in our lives.

When I said yes, the air felt full of excitement. As soon as I spoke, Evette, Elijah, and Lorenzo cheered. They rushed in, their energy adding to the joy of the moment. They hugged me and Christopher, forming a tight, happy group. The children's laughter filled the air, echoing our happiness.

Christopher's face shined with joy, his eyes sparkling with emotions as he hugged me and the children. His smile was wide and genuine, making even passersby smile at the heartwarming scene. The afternoon sun, now lower in the sky, cast a golden glow over us, bathing the park in the warm light that seemed to highlight our new beginning. The way everything was set up was the sweetest. When Christopher asked me to marry him, I felt like the happiest girl alive.

On the opposite side of the park, I noticed Pastor George and his wife approaching, along with other members of the congregation. That was when I put two and two together when I noticed the extra wine glasses and grape juice in the cooler. This was the best engagement party, and all of the people I love and adore most were there to witness a beautiful new beginning of the sweetest love story ever known. I knew at that moment, I had found the one that was truly meant for me.

Later I found out Christopher had involved Emma, all of the children, and our church family in his proposal plan. He wanted to make sure the kids felt they had a part of this new chapter in all of our lives. He knew how important family was to me and he wanted to honor that by making the proposal a family event. For the wedding plans, Christopher wanted to include our children, giving them very special jobs.

Lorenzo, his spirited young son, and Elijah, with his gentle nature, were given a very special job. They were to hold the rings, a task they took very seriously, I might add as they practiced their parts with excitement and seriousness every day up until our wedding day. The idea of being 'ring bearers' had them absolutely thrilled, and they talked about their roles with dedication. They were eager to make sure everything went perfectly.

Evette, with her bright and caring personality, was chosen to be the flower girl. Christopher had explained that her role would be more than just tossing petals; she was to help set the mood for the occasion, a role she embraced with enthusiasm. She then spent time running through the field picking the beautiful wildflowers from around the park and arranging them with care in her small hands.

Including Lorenzo, and the twins in this way not only strengthened our bonds but also showed Christopher's commitment to being part of a family built on love, support, and togetherness. They played quietly, sometimes glancing over with excited anticipation. The picnic spread was simple but thoughtful, with some of their favorite treats that Christopher knew I liked a lot.

They all had a special sparkle in their eyes, a mix of joy and a little hint of mischief, showing they were in on a delightful secret. The atmosphere was filled with love and anticipation. As we all mingled amongst one another, we could tell the children's excitement was clear, and their involvement made the moment even more meaningful for me. It was clear that this wasn't just about two people coming together but about a family becoming closer, with each member of our church playing a key role, sharing excitement as we built our shared future.

After they enjoyed a light meal, filled with laughter and gentle teasing, something changed.

The rest of the day was spent celebrating under the oak tree. We spread out the remaining picnic food, which now tasted even sweeter after the proposal.

Christopher and I shared stories of our first impressions of each other, making the children giggle and whisper in awe. We talked about the little moments that had strengthened our bond—the supportive phone calls, the family outings, and the quiet evenings spent together.

As we reminisced, we also started to dream about our future. We discussed possible wedding venues, the kind of ceremony we wanted, and even honeymoon ideas that would be fun for the whole family. Each shared vision built upon the last, creating hopes and plans for the years ahead.

Our laughter and voices mixed with the rustling leaves and occasional bird songs, which created the perfect soundtrack to the afternoon. The park, with its vibrant fall colors, felt like a witness to our joy, and the setting sun seemed to pause, giving us more time to savor our engagement.

This spontaneous celebration under the oak tree, surrounded by nature and bathed in golden sunlight, was more than just an engagement party—it was a promise of unity, support, and love. We promised to walk together through all of life's challenges and adventures. As the day ended, we packed up our belongings, our hearts full and spirits high, ready to step into the future together as a family.

This proposal was more than a simple agreement to marry—it marked the beginning of a new chapter for Christopher and me. It was a commitment not just to each other but to a future where our lives would be deeply intertwined, creating a blended family rooted in love, respect, and mutual understanding.

As we stood under the fading light, surrounded by the park's beauty and our children's excitement, Christopher and I felt a deep sense of unity. We were not just planning a wedding; we were building a new home—a place where each member could grow, feel supported, and thrive. This new home would be grounded in the shared values we had discussed over the past year: honesty, support, faith, and unconditional love.

We looked forward to creating a space where Lorenzo, Evette, and Elijah could feel equally cherished and valued, and where their individual needs and dreams were nurtured. Christopher and I talked about the importance of keeping open communication, where we could gather around the dinner table each night to share our day's experiences and challenges, supporting each other through life's ups and downs.

We also dreamed of holidays and family traditions that would blend our backgrounds and create new memories. Christmas mornings filled with laughter, Thanksgiving dinners with family and friends, and summer vacations where we could explore new places together. Each of these moments would strengthen our bonds, weaving a richer, more colorful family life.

Moreover, our union was built on a foundation of deep respect for each other's pasts and the paths that had led us to one another. I admired Christopher's dedication to his son and his kind nature, while Christopher was drawn to my resilience, nurturing spirit, and commitment to my children. Together, we knew this foundation would help us face any challenges with strength and grace.

As we got ready to start this journey together, Christopher and I felt very hopeful. We knew the road ahead would have challenges, but we had built a strong partnership that could face anything. With each shared dream and plan we made, we added another piece to the foundation of a future filled with love, unity, and endless possibilities. We stepped forward into this new chapter with open hearts, ready to face whatever came our way, together as a family.

NINETEEN

The sanctuary of Abundant Life Church had been turned into a place of calm beauty, showing my good taste and Christopher's wish for a wedding that was both special and personal. The decorations were simple but very pretty, with each piece chosen to make the place feel calm and graceful.

White ribbons, soft and gentle, decorated each pew. They fluttered as a light breeze came through the open doors. These ribbons, tied in neat bows, added a charming touch to the wooden pews, which also had bunches of fresh flowers. The flowers were in shades of soft white, cream, and green, matching the colors of the season. These colors were chosen for their calmness and to show peace and a new start, which is what our wedding was about.

As the sunlight came through the beautifully designed windows, the sun shone brightly, casting patterns of light across the aisle and onto the guests as they took their seats. The effect was amazing, making a mosaic of light on the floor and walls, adding to the heavenly feel of the place. This play of light seemed to bless the occasion, filling the space with a warm glow that felt almost magical.

This setting was not just a backdrop but a key part of the ceremony, adding to the emotional and spiritual meaning of the event. It was as if the church itself was celebrating with us, its walls and windows sharing in our joy. The mix of natural beauty from the flowers, the pure white ribbons, and the colorful light from the stained glass created a place that was not only beautiful to see but also deeply touching. This lovely setup made the perfect stage for Christopher's and my vows, making our moment of union even more special and memorable.

As the wedding day went on, guests began to arrive at Abundant Life Church, each stepping into a sanctuary filled with the sweet sound of a string quartet. The quartet, playing near the entrance, played classical songs that softly filled the air, creating a feeling of elegance and excitement. The choice of music was perfect, with tunes that ranged from delicate harmonies to rich, deep chords, making an atmosphere that was both uplifting and calm.

The welcoming tunes set a happy and expectant tone, as family and friends, dressed in their finest clothes, entered the church. Their faces lit up with smiles as they heard the beautiful music and saw the lovely decorations. There was a buzz of quiet excitement, and a soft hum of conversation as guests greeted each other and shared their joy for Christopher's and my special day. They whispered good wishes to each other, their voices blending with the music.

As they took their seats, many couldn't help but admire the decorations—the way the light shone through the stained glass windows, the pretty ribbons and flowers on the pews. Each part was noticed and loved, with guests pointing out their favorite details and talking about the overall beauty of the place.

This gathering was more than just a formality; it was a coming together of hearts and souls who had watched our love story grow. The music from the string quartet filled the space not only with sound but also with emotion, capturing the shared excitement of everyone there. It was a perfect start to the ceremony, setting a tone of seriousness and celebration that matched the importance of the occasion. This moment, full of emotion and beauty, was a fitting beginning to a day that promised to be filled with love, commitment, and shared happiness.

At the front of Abundant Life Church, Pastor George stood with a calm and kind presence, a symbol of spiritual guidance and care. As guests settled into their seats, his warm, welcoming manner reminded us of the journey that had brought us to this special day. Pastor George had been more than just a spiritual leader to us; he had been a mentor, a friend, and a key figure in our lives, especially as we found our way to each other.

Throughout our relationship, Pastor George had given us not only spiritual guidance but also practical help and heartfelt advice. His deep understanding of our lives and his wise words had helped us build a bond based on respect and shared faith. His role in our lives made his presence at the altar even more meaningful—it showed the trust and respect we had for him.

Having Pastor George officiate our wedding was a deeply meaningful choice for both Christopher and me. It was his teachings, after all, that often reminded us of the importance of kindness, patience, and unconditional love—qualities that defined our relationship. As Pastor George stood prepared to start the ceremony, we felt thankful for his part in guiding us to this important moment.

As he looked over the gathering, his eyes shining with pride and joy, Pastor George got ready to lead Christopher and I in our vows. This was not just a formality for him; it was a celebration of love and commitment that he had helped grow. His presence added a layer of depth and sincerity to the ceremony, making the vows more meaningful. This made the ceremony not just a union of two people, but a reaffirmation of our journey together under his guidance—a journey that was now blossoming into a lifelong commitment.

As the ceremony started, Evette, dressed in a delicate white dress with a floral crown on her curls, took her role as the flower girl seriously. She walked down the aisle, scattering petals with grace, her steps careful and proud. Following her were Elijah and Lorenzo, both serving as ring bearers. They walked side by side, holding a small pillow together, each smiling with pride and feeling important about their shared task. Their outfits matched the groom's, making them look just like Christopher's special attendants.

Then I made my entrance, looking radiant, thanks to Emma. I wore a flowing gown of soft ivory, with lace details that added a timeless elegance. My hair was styled in a simple updo, adorned with a few delicate flowers, and my smile lit up the room as I walked down the aisle. Emma, my bridesmaid and supportive sister, followed, dressed in a tasteful gown that matched the wedding's colors.

Christopher stood at the altar, looking poised and ready in his classic black tuxedo. As he waited for me to walk down the aisle, his posture showed quiet strength and readiness. His outfit was carefully chosen, the sharp lines of the tuxedo complementing his stature, making him the perfect groom. The black fabric stood out against the soft, warm light of the church, highlighting his presence at the altar.

His eyes, filled with emotion, watched eagerly for the first glimpse of me. As I began my walk, visible at the entrance of the sanctuary, Christopher's emotions surged. A tear ran down his cheek, silently showing the depth of his feelings. His face, usually composed, now openly showed the overwhelming joy and love he felt for the woman about to join him in marriage.

The connection between Christopher and I was strong as I walked toward him. It was as if an electric current ran through the air, linking us heart to heart. Our love was not just a feeling; it was a vivid, living force that seemed to fill the sanctuary. Guests could feel the intensity of our bond, a clear display of affection and commitment that filled the space with warmth and sincerity.

As I drew closer, the look in Christopher's eyes spoke volumes about our shared journey and the future we were about to start together. This moment, so full of emotion and meaning, resonated throughout the sanctuary, touching the hearts of all who watched it. The sight of Christopher, so visibly moved by the sight of his bride, underscored the profound love and mutual respect that formed the foundation of our relationship.

Pastor George began the ceremony with a warm welcome and a brief reflection on our journey, emphasizing our commitment, faith, and the blending of our families. The exchange of vows was deeply personal, with both Christopher and me sharing heartfelt promises and commitments, our voices steady but filled with emotion.

After the ceremony, the reception took place in the church's large hall, transformed into a beautiful celebration space. Tables were covered with elegant white table cloths and gold centerpieces featuring the same soft white and gold runners on the pews from the ceremony. The atmosphere was lively yet elegant, with the string quartet giving way to a live band that played a mix of classic hits and soft romantic songs.

The reception was filled with celebration and joy. As the evening began, Emma, the maid of honor, gave the first toast. She stood, glass raised, her voice clear and full of emotion, expressing her deep affection and hopes for me and Christopher. Her words were heartfelt, mixing humor with sentimentality, setting a tone of warmth and intimacy for the evening.

After Emma, a few of our closest friends from church took turns at the microphone. Each shared their own perspective on us, telling stories that brought laughter, nods of recognition, and even a few happy tears from the guests. These stories ranged from light-hearted misadventures and inside jokes to touching moments when we showed our care and commitment to each other and those around us.

The laughter that filled the room was often mixed with tears of joy, as friends and family celebrated the deep connection and love that Christopher and I shared. These stories did more than entertain; they painted a vivid picture of a couple who were not only partners to each other but also cherished members of a loving community. The stories told by the speakers showed how we had impacted the people around us, reminding us of the strong community and support we had built together.

As each person spoke, the bonds of friendship and family grew stronger. They shared memories and hopes for our future, making everyone feel closer. This part of the evening showed how much Christopher and I meant to our circle and how much they hoped for our future together. The mix of laughter and tears, stories and wishes, made the night emotional and special. It celebrated not just the union of two people but the coming together of families and friends in support and joy.

After the toasts, the focus shifted to dinner. The menu featured our favorite dishes, chosen to reflect our tastes and shared experiences. The food ranged from simple, comforting classics to more elaborate, gourmet options, all prepared by a local caterer known for their amazing cooking. The caterer worked closely with us to make sure the flavors were not only tasty but also meaningful, making the meal both a feast and a story.

The dining tables were set beautifully, with soft candlelight creating a warm, inviting glow. As plates were filled with delicious food, chatter and laughter filled the room. Guests enjoyed each bite, complimenting the thoughtful mix of flavors and the beautiful presentation. With chicken marsala, beef tips, pasta, a salad bar and dinner rolls on the menu, the food was not just filling; it was a key part of the celebration, bringing people together in shared enjoyment.

Amid the clinking of glasses and happy conversations, Christopher and I walked around the room. We approached each table with genuine warmth, spending moments with family and friends to personally thank them for their love and support. Each interaction was filled with smiles and heartfelt thanks, often sharing brief stories about our connection with each guest or group.

This mingling was not just a formal gesture but a sincere thank you to each person for their role in our lives. Our approach made each guest feel valued and appreciated, strengthening the feeling of togetherness and belonging that was clear throughout the ceremony. As we moved through the room, our gratitude was evident, and our happiness spread, making each guest feel closely connected to the joy of the occasion.

The reception reached its peak when it was time for our first dance. As the band started playing our chosen love song, "Goodness of God", a hush fell over the room. This song was special to us, filled with memories and meaning from our relationship. Under a canopy of twinkling lights, we stepped onto the dance floor.

Christopher and I danced together in perfect harmony, our steps practiced but filled with spontaneous joy from our deep connection. As we danced, our eyes stayed locked on each other, each gaze showing love, promise, and a shared future. The beauty of the moment was clear, as if the world around us had disappeared, leaving just the two of us in our shared bliss.

Surrounded by the soft glow of the lights and the gentle melody, our dance was a powerful show of our love and commitment. The scene was enchantingly beautiful, the kind that stays in the memories of all who saw it. As the song continued, our movements told a story of mutual respect, deep affection, and a journey of coming together through various challenges.

Inspired by the intimacy and affection in our dance, other couples began to join us on the dance floor. Friends, family, and loved ones paired up, drawn into the spirit of the moment. The dance floor quickly filled with couples, each moving to the music, celebrating not only our union but also the love and connections among all present. The dance showed how happy we were as a group, making us feel even closer and more loving, just like we were all one big family celebrating together on our wedding day.

As the evening began to wind down, one of the last ceremonial acts was cutting the wedding cake. The cake was a magnificent three-tiered masterpiece, elegantly designed to capture the essence of the day. Each layer was delicately crafted, showcasing smooth, pristine icing that gleamed under the soft lighting of the reception hall. Fresh flowers, carefully arranged, adorned the cake, echoing the blooms of my bridal bouquet. The colors and textures of the flowers added natural elegance to the cake, making it not just a dessert but a central decorative piece of the celebration.

With smiles and meaningful glances, Christopher and I approached the cake table, hand in hand. Guests gathered around, their cameras ready, eager to capture this sweet, symbolic moment. We took the cake knife together, our hands overlapping, and made a gentle cut through the soft layers of the cake. The room filled with applause and cheers, a shared expression of joy and festivity.

After carefully placing the first slice on a plate, we playfully fed each other a bite of the cake. Our actions were filled with laughter and gentle teasing, a light-hearted moment that showed our relationship perfectly. Feeding each other wasn't just a tradition; it was a promise of mutual support and love, made even sweeter by the joy of our wedding day.

This moment, filled with laughter and the sweetness of cake, was a perfect end to the formal part of our wedding celebration. It reminded everyone of the fun and happy moments of life we would share together, setting a tone of happiness and togetherness for our future. As we finished the last bites of cake, we shared a kiss, cheered on by our loved ones, ending the celebration on a sweet and joyful note.

Our wedding was more than just a typical event. It wasn't just about us getting married but about bringing together our families, friends, and communities. The day was full of love and laughter, from the early morning preparations to the last dance of the evening.

Every part of the ceremony and reception was chosen to show not only our love for each other but also our commitment to our families. Having Evette, Elijah, and Lorenzo as part of the ceremony showed this union, highlighting the merging of our lives into one family. Friends and family from different times in our lives came together, celebrating not just a wedding but the forming of new bonds and strengthening of old ones.

The air was filled with laughter, from the joyful chuckles during the toasts to the lighthearted banter around the dinner tables. Each laugh was a note in the symphony of joy that the day became. And amid the festivities, the promise of future happiness echoed, a sentiment shared by all who attended. They saw in us a partnership that promised not only to endure but to flourish, bringing joy not just to ourselves but to all who knew us.

Our wedding was full of love, hope and joy, a sign of what our future might be—full of happy years. As the party ended, we looked at our friends and family, and felt thankful. We knew this day was the start of a beautiful life together, filled with shared happiness, challenges, and successes. We were beginning a journey together, supported by the love of our families and community because I chose faith over fear.

www.ingramcontent.com/pod-product-compliance
Lightning Source LLC
Chambersburg PA
CBHW071141170626
46809CB00002B/722